Marilyn and Me

SHANTA EVERINGTON

Cinnamon Press
Independent Innovative International

Published by Cinnamon Press
Meirion House
Glan yr afon
Tanygrisiau
Blaenau Ffestiniog
Gwynedd LL41 3SU
www.cinnamonpress.com

The right of Shanta Everington to be identified as author of this work has been asserted by her in accordance with the Copyright, Designs and Patent Act, 1988. © 2007 Shanta Everington
ISBN 978-1-905614-17-2

British Library Cataloguing in Publication Data. A CIP record for this book can be obtained from the British Library

Designed and typeset in Garamond by Cinnamon Press
Cover design by Mike Fortune-Wood from original artwork supplied by dreamstime.com

Acknowledgements

A very big thank you to Jan Fortune-Wood and the rest of the team at Cinnamon Press for helping Marilyn's story see the light of day. I'm also indebted to Heather Beck, Ali Cargill, Heather Nelson, Ugo Pellizon, Yasmin Sooltan-Conway, Glenis Stott and Naomi Young from Manchester Metropolitan University Writing School and to my agent, Eve White. And last, but certainly not least, to my family - my husband, Raymond, son, Etienne, Mum, Dad and sisters, Kika and Krista - you are everything.

The quote from Paula Strasberg is from Susan Strasberg's biography, *Marilyn and Me* and is used with kind permission from Paula and John Strasberg.

Marilyn and Me

This book is a tribute to all the people who allowed me to support them when I worked in community care.

"After all, normal is not necessarily good, it's just a numerical statistic that describes what most people are."

Paula Strasberg on Marilyn Monroe

Bus Stop

1

My name is Marilyn, like Marilyn Monroe. I was left for dead at a bus stop on Christmas Eve. In the newspaper that Mum brought in, I was plain Jane again: a retard with mousy brown hair and big glasses. That picture was taken before I got to bleach my hair and choose my own clothes and be who I wanted.

In my locker in the day centre, I have a poster of Marilyn Monroe pinned up. The one in the white dress, where it's blowing up in the air and she's laughing. I chose it because I thought she looked nice and it made me smile every morning when I opened the locker and because I wanted to be like her: pretty and happy and normal.

I'm twenty-five years old and I have a learning disability. At the day centre, I'm in the singing group and do dancing and hair and make-up. My key worker is Sharon, who taught me how to do my washing and sort it into colours. I like sorting things into colours. Sharon's got lots of colours in her hair. She's nice and she's Billy's key worker too. Billy's hair is black. I wasn't attacked by Billy. Billy is my friend and he came to visit me in hospital with Sharon but I pretended to be asleep so no visitors were allowed in except Mum and the doctors and nurses. I don't know why I did that. Billy is my friend. But my head was hurting and all I wanted to do was hide, so I pulled the sheet over my head and screwed my hands into fists.

Mum is sitting next to my bed. I can smell her perfume. It's called Charlie Red and it comes in a red bottle. I don't like it much but it's better than the other smells here. You can smell bleach. Mum uses lots of bleach to keep things clean and hygienic. It's very important to keep things clean and hygienic. But you can still smell the smells of people being ill, like if you are sick in a bucket next to your bed and no-one takes it away and it stinks. You can smell food as well but it's not a nice smell to make you hungry. It's like leftovers or the bin.

I don't think I've been here very long but more than a day. I'm not very good at the time, so I don't know. If you put your dinner in the oven at the start of Coronation Street, it will be ready at the end. That's what Sharon taught me. You can use sand timers if you get confused with numbers. Or you can do two things at the same time, like putting your washing in the washing machine on a short wash and a boil-in-the-bag in a pan of water. When the washing finishes, the food is cooked. Everything is different here, so I get confused. The nurses wake you up really early and people bring food on trays when you're not even hungry. But maybe I have been here for a long time because I just remembered that I wasn't allowed any food first of all. Mum said they had to feed me through a tube, like a hosepipe but smaller. They don't put real food down it but a special liquid with something called nutrients.

'My poor baby. My poor baby Jane.' Mum strokes my forehead but I keep my eyes shut tight.

When I was twenty, I decided I wanted to be called Marilyn, like Marilyn Monroe. She used to be called Norma Jeane but she changed it to Marilyn when she was twenty because that was the start of her new life and she could forget about all the bad things that had happened before. That's what I wanted too. Rose, my social worker, said it was up to me. Rose says that I am an adult and I can make my own choices.

Mum didn't like my new name but she got used to it because I wouldn't answer to Jane any more. When I was twenty-one, Rose got me a flat in Cranley Crescent in Southend. It's near the beach and the shops and it's very nice. Natasha came every day to help me learn how to do things myself. Now she just comes twice a week. It was best for me and best for Mum because we were shouting at each other a lot then. But she doesn't want me to go back to Southend.

8

She wants me to stay with her in Dagenham.

'My poor little Jane.'

I want to go home soon and go to sleep in my own bed. In my own flat. My bed is lovely and soft with three pillows. I have four sets of bed clothes that I bought with Natasha. They are four different colours - pink, peach, lilac and cream. I change them every week. The colours help me to remember.

Mum strokes my forehead but I keep my eyes shut tight. Mum says when I get better she's going to take me home and look after me. She says it was a mistake letting me live in Cranley Crescent with those liberals. It should never have been allowed. A terrible mistake. She says she doesn't know if she'll be able to cope with me at home, though. She'll have to see how it goes. I could always move into a nice little nursing home like Mrs. Tulser from number forty-five, where they have experienced nurses to look after you twenty-four hours a day and not let you out of their sight so you can't get into trouble. She says it would be safe. It might be for the best.

She keeps on stroking and talking but I keep my eyes shut tight. Then the nurse comes in and tells Mum I need sleep and Mum kisses me on the head and I keep my eyes shut tight.

At the beginning, there were two of me. That's what Mum told me once a long time ago when she was crying. I haven't forgotten but I think I'm supposed to have. She said it was called twins. Two people who are the same. Sometimes they wear the same clothes and have the same hair in pigtails, like Emma and Sally who used to live in our road when I was little but moved away when they were ten. Sometimes twins are two girls or two boys but sometimes they are a boy and a girl, which doesn't make sense because a boy and a girl are not the same.

But the other one of me died when she was coming out of Mum's body, so she didn't get a name and we're not supposed

9

to talk about her. There's a thing like a rope that joins the baby to the mum and sometimes things go wrong and it gets twisted and that can be dangerous. It was dangerous when we were born because one of us died and I nearly got strangled with the rope. They think that's why I'm the way I am. When you get strangled by a rope, your brain gets starved of oxygen. It needs oxygen like you need to breathe oxygen in the air and if it gets starved of oxygen, it might stop working properly. This is what happened to me.

Mostly my brain works okay. There are people a lot worse off than me. Mum told me that too. Some people can't even talk or move. Mum calls those people vegetables but Sharon says that's not a very nice thing to say because they are still people and have feelings even if they can't talk or move. Sharon says that they can still communicate and show their feelings by blinking an eye or something but it sounds very hard to me. Some people can't talk properly with words but they can still talk with noises and move around, like John and Susan at the day centre.

John and Susan live in a home like the one Mum was talking about. A home where you just have a room like a hospital and nurses look after you. There are homes for people like John and Susan who can't talk or do things for themselves and there are homes for old people like Mrs. Tulser. I do not want to live in a home. I have my own home in Cranley Crescent. It's a flat with its own bathroom with a blue bath and kitchen with a microwave and Natasha comes to visit me and help me but no-one has to live there with me. Mum is cross with Natasha. She says that Natasha didn't look after me properly and that's why I got attacked. I like Cranley Crescent because I know all the people who live in the flats there - Penny and Gillian, Billy, Nigel, Frank and Joan and Paul.

Sometimes I think about the other one of me. Sometimes I talk to her in my head. I call her Janey because she is the other one of me, who didn't get to change her name and start again. She didn't even get one name but I've got two. I might sing her a song. I might sing her a lullaby when I'm going to sleep. In your head, you can sing loud and no-one knows. It won't stop anyone else going to sleep. You can say anything you want. You can swear and shout and say bad things but if you say them out loud, you can get into trouble.

If she hadn't died, what would she be like? She would be like me but she might be worse off than me if the rope strangled her more because maybe her brain would work less. If you had a twin, you'd never be on your own. If you're on your own all the time, it can be very lonely but if you're with people all the time, it can make you cross. You might argue about noise and television and mess and sharing the bathroom. If I lived in a home like John and Susan, I would never have quiet time. I like to have quiet time, when you can think.

It must be very strange to meet yourself. Like looking in a mirror. I haven't looked in a mirror since I came in here because I'm scared to. I must look bad because Mum cried when she saw me. I don't think she's stopped crying since it happened.

2

Marilyn Monroe never had a baby. She had a husband but they got divorced. His name was Jimmy and she married him when she was sixteen. After Jimmy, she got married again. I would like to have a husband and a baby. It must be nice to have someone to love and to love you back. If I had a baby, I would love it and never give it away. I would never give it to someone else to take care of. People say I can't even look after myself, let alone a baby but that's not true. I would feed it and change it and give it a bath and wind it and sing it lullabies, like I sing to Janey. I'm good at singing.

When I was born, Mum was scared because of what the doctors told her. She didn't know how I'd turn out. She didn't know if she could cope with me. So she gave me to her sister, Maggie who lived in Southend. Aunt Maggie couldn't have children because her body didn't work properly. Maybe that's why she didn't mind that I didn't work properly either.

Aunt Maggie didn't even have a husband because he left before she got me but it didn't matter. I don't remember her that much but she must have loved me and I loved her. She died when I was four. Someone crashed into her car when she was driving home from the supermarket. I was strapped in the back. They say it's a miracle that I was okay. I don't remember it but I don't like cars. I always get the bus. But maybe now I don't like buses either because of what happened at the bus stop but I don't want to think about that.

After Mum's gone, I ask the nurse if I can look in the mirror. She has blonde hair like me but she doesn't have roots. Her hair is clean and shiny and she wears it in a pony tail. She says I have to talk to someone first. A man comes to talk to me. He's wearing a white coat and he has grey hair on his head and his eyebrows so he must be a doctor. He says my face looks a lot worse than it is. He says I might have scars, though. Do I know what scars mean? I do know what scars mean because I have a long thin one on my leg where I burnt myself when Barbara was my mum. I nod to show him that I do know.

He says they might be able to do something about the scars later but they want to see how it heals first. I understand because sometimes things look bad but then they look okay after. Like when Billy cut his finger at the day centre doing cooking and it looked like all the blood in his body was coming out of his finger and he screamed and then I screamed and even Sharon looked scared. But when he took the plaster off the next day, it was only a tiny cut and his finger had gone all crinkly.

Billy is a nice man. He is my friend. The nurse told me that he's come to visit again and this time I let him and Sharon in. Mum has gone home to get some rest but she'll be back. I watch the nurse talking to Billy and Sharon outside my room. I have my own room, not a bed on the ward. I look through my window. It is getting dark outside but I don't know what time it is. They haven't brought any food for a long time.

The door opens and Sharon comes in first. She swallows hard.

'How are you feeling, Marilyn?' She speaks in a very quiet voice.

Billy makes a noise like a horse and starts rocking. Billy is a rocking horse.

'Oh, I guess you must be pleased to see us?'

I'm laughing at the rocking horse joke. It makes my face hurt.

'My face hurts,' I say and I start to cry. The tears sting and make it hurt worse.

'Oh, oh. Shall I get the nurse?' asks Sharon.

'No,' I shout. 'I don't want the nurse.'

'Okay,' says Sharon. 'Billy, come and say hello to Marilyn.'

Billy is facing the wall. He is still rocking. He is crying too. I know it is because I look very bad and he is scared. I want

13

him to stop being scared.

'It's alright, Billy,' I say. 'Come and sit down.'

He is still making the noise but it is quieter now and he turns round.

'Come on, Billy,' says Sharon, patting a chair.

Billy steps forward, then back again, then forward and he sits on the chair. He stares at me. I look at his face. It is all puffy. His eyes are very wet and there are lots of red lines in them. But they are not as bad as mine. We look at each other's eyes. Billy is quiet. He blinks but doesn't say anything. I wonder if the blinks mean anything. He looks at my forehead, my nose, my cheek, my mouth, my chin. He looks away.

I start to cry.

He looks at the tubes coming out of my arm. He looks at the machines that make whirring sounds. He looks at the flowers that Mum brought in. Red roses. Like a man might buy you for Valentines' Day, if he loves you. He looks at the newspaper next to the vase on the bedside table. The one with the picture of plain Jane inside.

He puts his hand on my hand.

It is quiet.

'So how are you feeling?' asks Sharon.

Bad. I am feeling bad.

I say, 'I want to go home,'

Billy looks up at me again. Then he looks at Sharon.

'Can Marilyn go home?' he asks her.

'I don't know,' says Sharon. 'What did the doctors say?'

I shrug.

'They said there might be scars. I don't care. I can put make-up on them.'

'Have you spoken to your mum about going home?'

I pull my hand away from Billy and hit the bed. It makes him jump.

'I want to go home to my flat!' I can hear that my voice is loud.

'Okay,' says Sharon and I think this means I can go home. Then she says, 'Have you spoken to Rose about it?'

I shake my head.

'What about Natasha?'

'No!' I don't mean to shout but it comes out very loud and the nurse opens the door. She is small and she has red spiky hair and lots of gold earrings in each ear. I don't remember her. Where is the nurse with the silky blonde ponytail?

'I think Jane's had enough for now,' she says. 'Maybe you can come back tomorrow.'

I want to tell the nurse with the red hair that my name is Marilyn not Jane.

But I don't.

3

'What day is it?' I ask her.

She laughs and her earrings jingle jangle. Like Christmas. I count them. There are five rings in each ear. Five gold rings. Four turtle doves. Three French hens. Two, two what? Two turtle doves? Then what's four?

'It's New Year's Eve, Poppet.'

I wonder how old she is. She must dye her hair that colour. She looks young and old at the same time. She has lines on her forehead like Mum. But Mum wouldn't wear that many earrings. She wears big gold hoops when she goes out.

New Year's Eve.

'How many days is that after Christmas?'

'Seven days. You've been here a week, Poppet. I don't suppose you remember the first few days, do you? You were in a bad way.'

She's standing very close to the bed and she's looking at a clipboard like the one that Sharon uses at the day centre to clip her recipe cards on. Pizzas are brown for the base, red for tomato, green and orange for peppers, white for onion and yellow for cheese.

Left for dead. That's what Mum said. I was left for dead at a bus stop on Christmas Eve. I think this means I have missed Christmas Day. I was going to Joan and Paul's for Christmas dinner. Turkey, roast and all the trimmings. Billy was coming too and Penny and Gillian. Mum was spending Christmas Day with her boyfriend, Steve. Steve is a builder and he makes Mum happy. But sometimes they fight. Steve lives with Mum in Dagenham. I don't like Dagenham. It is grey and there is no sea, just lots of blocks of flats that are very high. Southend is much better. You can walk along the pier and throw pebbles in the sea.

I was left for dead on Christmas Eve. I was in a bad way.

'Am I in a good way now?' I ask the nurse with red hair.

She checks the clipboard.

'You're getting there, Poppet,' she says and smiles at me.

'My name's Marilyn,' I tell her.

'Oh.' She checks the clipboard again. 'Your chart says Jane.'

'Yes but my name's Marilyn. I changed it to Marilyn.'

'Okay, Marilyn.'

'What's your name?'

'My name's Gail, Poppet. I mean, Marilyn.' She smiles again. She looks nice when she smiles.

'What was I like when I got here?'

'You were in a bad way.' The creases in her forehead squash together and she looks down. Then she looks back at me. 'Now the swelling's going down on your face, I can see you are a very pretty girl.'

'Can I wash my hair? And have a bath?'

I am in a small room on my own and there is a little bathroom in the corner and it smells of Dettol which is good because it means it is clean. It's important to be clean and hygienic. When I want to go to the toilet, I have to pull a cord so a nurse can help me get out of bed. I have been here for seven days. I must have been to the toilet lots of times in seven days. Mum said I had to go in the bed because I couldn't get up because I was in too much pain. That's when they were feeding me through the tube. I don't remember it. The nurse has been giving me bed baths but it is horrible and I want a proper bath. It's important to be clean and hygienic.

'Yes, Poppet. I should think so. We'll have to check your dressings. I can help you wash your hair. It'll be a shower not a bath.'

Gail clips the clipboard on the end of the bed. She is wearing a gold wedding ring to match her gold earrings. Gail has a husband.

There isn't a bath in the bathroom. Not like my blue bathroom at Cranley Crescent. Gail helps me to get into the bathroom. There are rails on the wall, like at Frank's flat. I

17

am wearing a nightdress that I don't remember putting on. There is a shower. It has a white plastic seat with holes in it so you can sit down while you have a shower and the water goes through the holes. Frank has a shower with a seat in his flat at Cranley Crescent. I went in his bathroom to go to the toilet once when I was round his flat. Frank is quite old. He said the seat makes it easier because he doesn't have to worry about slipping and it's too hard to get in and out of the bath. I want a bath.

'Don't they have baths here?' I ask Gail.

'It's mainly showers,' she replies. 'This room has disabled access so it has a special shower.'

'I have a bath in my flat. I don't need that shower. I can use a bath.'

I don't want to use that stupid shower. I don't want to put my bum on that seat that someone else's dirty bum has been on.

'There's no bath, Poppet.'

'My name is Marilyn and I want a bath.'

'Marilyn, we haven't got a bath here. It's a very good shower. You'll feel better after. How about you slip your nightdress off and I'll set the shower for you. We don't want it too hot, now.'

I have the shower but I keep my bum off the seat. Gail laughs. It's very difficult because I've got to be careful. Gail takes the dressings off my cuts and I have to keep some bits out of the water or do it gently because it hurts. I see purple and blue and red and yellow on my body. I don't remember seeing all these colours on my body before. Gail helps me wash my hair without getting shampoo in my face or eyes but I end up sitting on the chair after all and that makes me cry.

'Shall I help you get dry, Poppet?'

My name is Marilyn.

When Aunt Maggie died, I got a new mum and dad called Lynn and Terry but only for a little while because they were only foster parents not real parents. Foster parents can only keep you for a little while. Marilyn Monroe had foster parents too when she was little. My real mum came to visit me at Mummy Lynn's and shouted and then she didn't come back for a long time or maybe only a short time. Then I had another mum and dad after that called Barbara and Mike, and Mum came to see me again.

When she first came, she was sad but then she started laughing. She said I was funny. I was a funny girl. I said funny things. I did funny things. I don't know why I was funny but it made her laugh and that was good so she let me go and live with her in her house in Dagenham when I was nine.

Mum wasn't married to my dad. She says he was a bad man but she was too young to know any better. Marilyn Monroe got married to Jimmy when she was sixteen but she got divorced when she was twenty. I haven't even got a boyfriend but I have had boyfriends before. My favourite boyfriend was Jamie. My first boyfriend was Sam. He was my boyfriend when I was five and we held hands in the playground. He smelt of talcum powder and jelly. I went to his birthday party and he gave me a present even though it was his birthday. It was a game called Pass the Parcel and I won it. It was a puzzle of a lion and I still have it.

I like parties. Everyone is happy and has lots of fun. You get to dress up in nice clothes and do your hair and makeup. Girls wear dresses in all different colours. I was going to a party on Christmas Eve. Everyone was going. Joan and Paul, Penny and Gillian, Nigel and even Frank, who doesn't go out much. The party was at the day centre. Sharon was organising it. I was wearing a gold dress and red lipstick and I had washed my hair and put it in curlers with Natasha before Natasha went. It took me a long time to get my hair right after I took the curlers out and we were running late. Natasha had to go somewhere. I was supposed to get the bus with Joan and Paul and Penny and Gillian. We were all going to

19

get the bus together.

My favourite boyfriend was Jamie. He was my boyfriend when I was eighteen. He was very good-looking and I had sex with him lots of times in his bedroom. Sex is how you make a baby. If it's with your husband or someone you love and who loves you, it's called making love. If someone does it to you and you don't want it, it's called rape. Every woman has the right to say no, but some men think no means yes.

Once we did it in my bedroom in Dagenham and Mum came in and found us and got angry and threw him out and screamed at him and told him never to come near me again or she would call the police. But we weren't doing anything wrong. We were only having sex. That was when I started getting the injections that stop babies. But if I stop having the injections, maybe I can have a baby, one day. It's not fair because Mum and Steve have sex all the time and she's had lots of boyfriends before but she doesn't like me to have sex with anyone.

Gail let me borrow some lipstick on her way back from seeing the other patients. I put it on without looking.

'People will be going to parties tonight, won't they?' I asked her.

Last year, I went to the pub on New Year's Eve. Everyone went. There was a countdown for midnight. Ten, nine, eight, seven, six, five, four, three, two, one. Everybody kissed everybody else.

'Yes, I expect they will be,' said Gail.

'What about you?'

'Ah, no. Not me. I'll be here, tonight.'

'Doesn't your husband mind?'

Gail laughs. Then she smoothes down her skirt.

'Sometimes. This is my job. You can't pick and choose the shifts.'

'Will you have a party tomorrow?'

'Well, I don't know about a party but I'll be doing dinner

20

with Greg and the kids.'

'That's nice.'

I look in the mirror. The lipstick is the same colour as the cuts on my face. There are too many red lines. I wipe it off with the back of my hand.

'Ah, what did you do that for?' asks Gail.

'How old are your children?'

'Let me see now,' she laughs again. 'I have to think about that! Jenny's eleven and Jake's fourteen.'

'Are they clever?'

'Yes, yes, I suppose they are.'

Gail smiles when she talks about her children. That must mean that she loves them very much and they make her happy. She would never give them away to someone else.

'Who looks after them when you're at work?'

'Sometimes Greg, sometimes the childminder.'

Gail tells me about her childminder. She is called Sue. A childminder is someone who is paid to look after someone else's children. But not like foster parents. The childminder only looks after them when the mum and dad are at work and then the childminder goes home when the mum and dad get home. It is a job. My mum doesn't have a job. She gets money from the post office like me. But she doesn't have to go to a day centre. She can spend all her time with Steve or doing what she wants.

4

'I said I was going to visit, didn't I, Gillian, didn't I say? I did. Who wants to go? Who wants to go? Yeah. That'd be nice, wouldn't it? Shall we? Ha!'

Penny and Gillian have come to see me. They share a flat in Cranley Crescent. I want to go home to my flat in Cranley Crescent. I want to have a bath in my blue bathroom and make myself a cup of tea, just the way I like it, not like here.

'Happy New Year,' I say to them because today is New Year's Day and Gail has gone home to make dinner for her family. Mum hasn't been back since, since I don't know. Since before.

'Happy New YEEAAAARRR!! HA haaaaa!' says Penny.

She is leaning right over my bed and her spit goes in my face. She is being very loud and the nurse with the blonde ponytail peeps in the window to see what the noise is. Then she walks away. Penny has black hair, which is very greasy and is sticking up all round her head. I'm glad that I washed my hair with Gail yesterday even if I did have to put my bum on the seat that everyone else's bum had been on.

'Gillian! Gillian! She's here! She's here! Happy New Year! Ha, haaaaaaaaaaa!'

Gillian is still by the door. She looks scared like Billy did when he first came but she's not rocking or making a noise like Billy. She is standing very still and quiet and her eyes have gone very big. Her hair is not sticking up like Penny's. It is very thin and has no colour and it is close to her head.

'Oh, oh,' she says.

'Hello, Gillian.'

Penny is still talking.

'Do you want to sit down?' I ask Gillian.

'Oh, oh. Okay.'

But she doesn't sit down. She walks to the other side of

the bed and stands. She leans over very close and looks at me with her big eyes.

Penny looks up at her and carries on, '…and onions. Can't make it otherwise, can ya? Coronation Street on tonight. Who's gonna get the carrots? Never wanted to go. Can't make me, can they? They can't MAKE MEEEEEEEEEEEEEEEEEEE!!! I'll get them. Onions. Oh, potatoes too. GILLIAN!!!!'

They will be cooking dinner when they get home and watching TV. I wonder when I can go home and cook dinner. I want to eat a pizza in my flat. Sharon showed me and Billy how to make a pizza in cooking. First we went to *Sainsbury's* to buy the ingredients but some people were staring because Billy started doing his horse noise when someone bumped into him. You start with a frozen base and then spread on tomato stuff with a spoon and then chop up tomatoes and onions and green and orange peppers and then grate the cheese and sprinkle it over the top but not too much because cheese is full of fat. You can add herbs if you want. Sharon says that sometimes she puts banana on her pizza but that sounds horrible. Sharon showed me how to use the knife properly so that it's not dangerous. It wasn't the way Mum does it but Sharon knows the right way to do things. She has picture cards about using ovens and she let me take a set home so I can make pizza if I want.

'Yes, Penny,' says Gillian and she strokes my hair, smiling. 'What lovely hair. Lovely.'

As she strokes my hair, I can smell the smell of shampoo.

'Was the party good?' I ask them, moving my head from side to side, not sure which one to look at.

'Party? Party?' Penny is walking around now. 'Haaaaaaaa!! Ha, ha!!'

'On Christmas Eve,' I say. 'Did you go to one yesterday, too?'

'Yesterday?' says Gillian, looking confused. 'Oh, oh. Christmas?'

'The party at the day centre?'

They look at me like they don't know what I'm talking about. Then Penny takes a huge breath and says, 'Yeah, yeah! Christmas Eve! Lots of food, crisps, chocolate...'

'What happened to you?' asks Gillian. She is still stroking my hair. It feels nice so I close my eyes. Like when Mum was stroking my forehead. Only that wasn't nice because of the things she was saying. Mum and Steve will have gone to the pub, I bet. They will have done the countdown and kissed each other at midnight.

Jamie was my favourite boyfriend but not my last boyfriend. My last boyfriend was Keith. I don't know if he is still my boyfriend. Not after what happened. I was going to meet him at the party. I was going to look really nice for him, in my gold dress. I had matching sandals, with straps, in gold. Natasha said my feet would be cold but I wore tights. I had a gold bag too and gold earrings but only one pair, not like Gail. I did my makeup just right. I was looking in my Marilyn Monroe book and I painted on a beauty spot just like hers, like I always do when I go out.

I wish I could be her because everyone loved her and she was famous. She didn't have to go to a day centre but she could make lots of films and earn lots of money. She had a glamorous life. People say she was very unhappy but I don't see how that could be true. Maybe when she was little but not when she grew up and was wearing her white dress and laughing. Or maybe she did that to make herself feel better. If I am sad, I like to dress up and put on my makeup and my beauty spot and put on some music and dance in my living room in gold sandals. I think we would have got on well because we would understand about foster parents and things. But we wouldn't have to talk about them. We would just know. But we would talk about makeup and clothes and films and boys.

The best film that I like is *Gentlemen Prefer Blondes* and I think it is true. I only had one proper boyfriend when I had brown hair, and that was Jamie, but I've had lots and lots of boyfriends since I was blonde. Keith is a nice boyfriend but he's not as good at sex as Jamie. We've only done it once and I was his first time. He is younger than me so I call him my toy boy! Maybe I should find a boyfriend who is older. Keith is twenty-one and he lives with his mum and dad. I don't think they like me because when I went round for dinner, they looked at me like I had done something bad.

I had dressed up specially to meet them. Natasha said it's important to make a good impression when you meet your boyfriend's parents. I wonder if Natasha has a boyfriend. I don't think she does. When she comes to see me, she doesn't talk much about herself but sometimes she talks about a man called Seb. She lives with him but he's not her boyfriend. I think she would like him to be her boyfriend but he won't be because he has a boyfriend of his own. This is called being gay. If you are a woman and you have a girlfriend then you are gay or a lesbian.

Steve says it's disgusting. He said that when we were all watching TV at Mum's house and two men were kissing. He says it makes him want to puke to see two men kiss. I don't know what he thinks about two women kissing. I kiss my mum and I used to kiss Maggie and Mummy Lynn and Mummy Barbara but that was different. I can't imagine kissing a woman in that way because I like men too much.

Sharon says you should live and let live. I don't really know what this means because you have to live if you are alive and you have to let live unless you kill someone. I don't think Steve would actually kill someone for being gay but I don't really know because he has been in trouble with the police before and sometimes he hits Mum. I have seen her face when it was red and purple and yellow and when she had a black eye. She didn't look as bad as me but still quite bad. But she says Steve doesn't mean it and he makes her happy.

When I went to meet Keith's mum and dad, I was wearing

a really nice dress with flowers on and a new pink bra from *Marks and Spencer's* but Keith's dad kept looking at my bra because it was showing at the front. Not really bad like a slag but he kept looking and I think that made Keith's mum cross and so she didn't like me anymore. Keith's mum and dad are called Mr and Mrs Berry and they live in a big house. Mr Berry goes to work in a suit everyday and Mrs Berry looks after the house. I haven't been to the house since then but Keith has been to my flat in the day when he was supposed to be at college and I was supposed to be at the day centre.

Keith told me he loves me but it's a secret. We can't tell his mum because she doesn't understand and she wants him to love Lorraine, who lives in the same road as them and doesn't wear clothes that show her bra. Marilyn Monroe had lots of boyfriends. I bet they told her they loved her. I bet she didn't have to keep it secret. Unless they were married. If you go out with a married man it has to be a secret. Nobody is allowed to find out.

'We have to go now,' says Gillian.

I open my eyes but they are gone.

I am on my own again.

I am on my own.

Ladies of the Chorus

5

The curtain around my bed is blue and it has brown and yellow stains on it. I have been looking at it for a long time because there is nothing else to do and no-one to talk to, unless I go to the television room but I don't want to do that because when I went on New Year's Eve, it was boring and nobody spoke anyway. They just stared.

I've seen Mum, Billy and Sharon, Penny and Gillian but I haven't seen Keith or Natasha or Rose and I am very worried. I want Keith to visit to find out if he still loves me and is still my boyfriend. I need Natasha or Rose to visit to let me know when I can go home. I don't know if I want to see Mum today or not. I don't know if she will come.

'Hello, Poppet.'

Gail is back at work today. She had two days off. I know because I had two breakfasts. One on New Year's Day when Gail had dinner with her family and one on the next day when no-one came. They were porridge in a bowl on a tray. There were lots of other trays in between but I just counted breakfasts because you only have one breakfast a day.

'How are you feeling today?'

'When can I go home?'

Gail has got her arms folded in front of her chest. I think that means she is cross but I don't know why. That's what Mum does when she is cross with me. I don't want to go back to Dagenham and live with Mum and Steve. I don't like Dagenham and I don't like Steve even if he does make Mum happy. She can live with him. I don't have to.

'I don't know, Poppet. See what the doctor says later. Has your social worker been in yet?'

'No. When is she coming?'

Gail is not smiling today. She unfolds her arms and looks at the clipboard. I hate that clipboard.

'I don't know. Have you been crying, Poppet?'

'My name is Marilyn.'

I turn on my side so I don't have to look at Gail who is cross but I don't know why.

'I don't know, Marilyn. Do you want to be left in peace for a while?'

I hear the metal clip of the clipboard bash on the metal on the bed. I hear her shoes squeak as she walks out. I hear the door close. I feel the air come in. I pull the sheet over my head and I start to sing to Janey. Marilyn Monroe had a singing teacher to teach her how to sing in her films. She made a lot of films. I would like to make a film.

I am good at singing. I am in the singing group.

When I was at school, I was picked for the choir because the teacher said that I opened my mouth nice and wide like an 'O'. Sometimes, I used to open my mouth very wide like an 'O' but not let any noise out. I just pretended to be singing because I didn't want to sing it wrong. But the teacher picked me for the choir anyway. But now I am good at singing because I learned properly at the day centre. We sing in a group and we sung 'Bridge Over Troubled Water' and it made me cry. I sing very loudly when I am at home by myself and I sing quietly to Janey, like I am now.

There are lots of singers who look like Marilyn Monroe, like Madonna who even copied her beauty spot like I do. If I was a singer, I would look like her too and I would make sure my hair was always nice and blonde. Not like Madonna who lets it go dark. Marilyn had dark hair when she was Norma but she didn't let it go dark when she became Marilyn so I won't either. When I get out of here, I'm going to see Chrissie to get my roots done.

The newspaper is still on the bedside table. I bet Marilyn Monroe used to have her picture in the newspaper all the time. She had lots of photographs taken and she looks really pretty in all her pictures like the one on the side of my mug. It's white and the picture is just of her head. It came with a teaspoon with a tiny picture of her head on the end. I have lots of things with her on. I have a badge that says, 'Marilyn Monroe's Greatest Fan'. I have a pencil sharpener with her picture that I use for my eyeliners. I've got lots of calendars from all different years.

Mum showed me the newspaper. If my name and picture are in the paper, I wonder if that means I am famous. The words say, 'Handicapped girl left for dead at bus stop on Christmas Eve'. Underneath is the picture. It was taken on my eighteenth birthday. I am not smiling. I've got lots of spots. I am wearing a horrible black jumper. I don't have many photos of myself. I hate that picture. I wish it wasn't in the paper where everyone can see it. Dave took the photo. He used to be Mum's boyfriend but not anymore. He took the photo just after I'd had an argument with Mum on my birthday and she'd slapped me across the face.

Mum should have given them a nice photo of me for the paper. Like ones from the day centre when I am smiling and I've got my makeup on. She should have told them my name was Marilyn. She shouldn't have let them write handicapped because everyone knows that's not a nice word to call people even if it's not as bad as calling someone a vegetable. Sharon said we don't use the word handicapped anymore. But that's a lie because it says I am handicapped in the paper and everyone will read it.

My cheek is pressed against the bed and it feels sore. I touch my skin and it feels all funny and hard. I don't press it hard because it would hurt. If the scars don't go away, I can put makeup on them or maybe the doctors will do an operation on my face to make them go away. Mum is saving up to get her eyes done like Anne Robinson. Steve thinks it is a good idea because it will make her look younger. If the doctors give me an operation, I might ask them to make me look more like Marilyn Monroe.

I hear the door handle click. Gail must have decided that I've had enough peace and quiet. I turn over to face the door but I keep my eyes closed and wait for her to call me Poppet.

31

I smell Charlie Red.

'How's my poor Jane?'

'Jesus!' This is the first time Steve has come in with Mum.

'I told you, didn't I?' Mum says to him. 'And you think she can go back there? Well, do you? Do you?'

'I don't know what to say, Ange. Jesus Christ. I wasn't expecting… A black eye and a few bruises maybe. Shall I wait in the car?'

The door closes behind him and Mum is by the bed.

'Are you awake, Jane?' she asks.

I open my eyes and look at her. She's had her hair cut. It is very shiny and smooth. It swings above her shoulders.

'Happy New Year, Darling.'

'Happy New Year, Mum.'

She smiles so wide when I say that, as if she thinks it really means that I am happy.

'So…' Mum is fiddling with her bag. I know that means she wants a cigarette. 'Everything's going to be alright now. I promise you, Jane. I spoke to the doctor, this morning and he…'

'When can I go home?'

'He said he sees no reason why you shouldn't be able to come home next week. They'll have to sort something out for when you get home. We don't want Steve to have to keep driving you back up here…' Mum is talking very fast. I watch her mouth move. Her lipstick is red. Her lips are crinkly. They are stretched tight over her teeth. Her teeth are brown from too much smoking. She is still talking. I don't think red lipstick suits her. It makes her teeth look more brown. Maybe she should save up to get her teeth done as well as her eyes. 'So, what do you think?'

'When is Rose coming?'

'Rose? What's it got to do with Rose? You're coming back with me and Steve next week. The doctor says…'

When Rose comes, it will be okay. Rose says I am an adult and I can make my own decisions. Rose knows that Steve hits

Mum even though he makes her happy. Rose won't make me go back there.

'When is Rose coming?'

6

Rose is here. She has come to see me after ten days. Gail has put a calendar next to my bed and she crosses off each day for me with her biro, so I can count how many days I have been here and how many days until I go home. It has a picture of a white cat on it with blue eyes. I have a Marilyn Monroe calendar at home but I haven't got it with me because I didn't get to pack. Gail's son Jake is doing his GCSE subjects. Gail wants him to be a doctor when he grows up but he wants to be a footballer.

There is a red cross on 7 January because that's when the doctor said I should be able to go home. Rose is wearing a grey suit. I remember when Rose was wearing a long purple dress that showed the red rose tattoo on her shoulder and her hair was long loose red curls and I asked her if she had changed her name to Rose or if she was always called Rose. She was lucky because her mum called her Rose when she was born. Rose's name is right for her. She looks like a rose.

But not today. Today, she looks more like a pencil than a rose. I think they call it a pencil skirt because it is long and thin and maybe because it is grey like the colour a pencil writes in. All her lovely red hair is brushed up into a bun. Like a teacher or someone who works in a bank. This is how she dresses for meetings, especially the ones called Care Planning Meetings, like we had before I was allowed to move into Cranley Crescent.

Rose is called a Care Manager. She is very important. She is the most important person at the Care Planning Meetings because she is in charge. There are other people at meetings too, like Mum and Sharon and Natasha. Rose says I am in charge but I don't think this is right because not everyone listens to me but everyone listens to Rose. Rose listens to me. She is very good at listening, not like Mum. Rose says that social workers have to be good at listening. She is not my friend. She is my Care Manager.

Marilyn Monroe had lots of managers. A manager is important because they help you and sort things out for you and they can make other people do what you want. Marilyn Monore even married one of her managers. He was called Arthur. I'm not sure if you're allowed to do that. I don't think Marilyn Monroe was always happy with her manager because they didn't always help her. Sometimes people tried to make her do things she didn't want like take her clothes off for photos or act in films she didn't like and not in films she did like.

Rose has always been my Care Manager, since I became an adult when I was eighteen. When you are an adult you can do what you want and you don't have to do what your mum says. Rose says I am an adult and I can make my own decisions. Mum says you can't always get what you want. Mum says life isn't fair. She says life isn't always a bed of roses but I don't know if she says that because of Rose.

Marilyn Monroe's managers got her into modelling and films and stuff. They helped her learn how to sing and act and choose the right clothes. You have to have a manager if you are famous. It is different to the manager you get if you are disabled or have problems. They're just social workers but they call themselves managers. They only manage your care but sometimes they help you get jobs too, like Joan. Her Care Manager helped her get a job in a florist, which is a shop that sells flowers, but she didn't like it. She kept getting the flowers mixed up.

I've never had a job but I would like to have one maybe. But not if I have to get up too early because I am not very good at that.

'Marilyn?'

I think Rose has been talking to me but I didn't hear her. Mum wanted to come in with Rose but Rose said she wanted to talk to me by myself first.

'How can you tell the difference between a rose and a

carnation?'

'Marilyn, did you hear what I said?'

'Yes.'

'What did I say?'

Rose is clicking the end of her biro in and out. In and out.

'I know this is difficult for you, Marilyn. What has happened to you...'

'When can I go home?'

I see Gail walk past. I see her through the window. She looks in and smiles. Gail is my friend. I wonder if she'll let me come and have dinner at her house. Rose is not my friend. She is my Care Manager. You are not allowed to go to your Care Manager's house. It is called boundaries. People can get in trouble.

'Marilyn.' Rose says my name and she takes my hand in her hands. I look at her. She is wearing grey eye shadow to match her grey pencil suit. It is a grey day. 'You...'

'Why hasn't Natasha come to see me?' Natasha is my support worker. She isn't my Care Manager.

'Natasha feels very, very bad about what's happened.'

'Why?'

Natasha is nearly my friend but I know it is her job too. She gets paid to help me. But she says she likes being with me. We have a laugh together. When I first moved in Natasha came every day to help me learn how to do things myself. Now she just comes twice a week. Sometimes we go out. It is called social support but it means going to the cinema or to the pub. I've met her friends at the pub. Seb and his boyfriend Johnny are nice even if Steve says that gays are disgusting.

'Marilyn. You understand that it's Natasha's job to support you to live independently and make sure you are safe. She feels that she let you down because you weren't safe.'

Mum is cross with Natasha. She says that Natasha didn't look after me properly and that's why I got attacked. Mum is wrong.

'But it wasn't her fault!'

'Okay, okay.' Rose squeezes my hand.

'Anyone could get attacked.' I pull my hand away and I snatch up the newspaper. I throw it at Rose. 'Not just handicapped people. Anyone!'

'That's very true, Marilyn.' Rose is talking very quietly. She is very quiet and I am very loud.

'It's doesn't mean Natasha should get in trouble. I was supposed to get the bus with Joan and Paul and Penny and Gillian. I took too long with my hair. It was my fault!'

'It wasn't your fault that you were attacked,' says Rose but I am getting confused. 'It's very important that you understand that.' I don't know if I understand that. 'It was the fault of the boys who did it.'

'So when can I go home? When can I see Natasha?'

'The police are very concerned that these boys might do this again if they are not caught.'

I talked to a police woman before. Another social worker was there. I haven't met her before. The police woman asked me lots of questions like doing a test at school but I wasn't very good at the answers.

How many boys were there? What were they wearing? How old did they look? What colour was their hair? What colour was their skin? What colour were their clothes? How tall were they? What did they say? Did they have an accent? What did they do? Which boy did what?

They had white trainers. I told them they had white trainers. Dark clothes. They weren't wearing Christmas outfits. They didn't look as if they were going to a party.

How long were you at the bus stop? Did any buses stop when the boys were there? What number bus went past? Did you see any other people? Cars? What cars? What colours? Where did they take you?

I told the police I'm not very good at time or numbers. I saw a blue car and a white van go past. I saw a black dog being walked. He was small and fluffy and I think he had a red collar. I don't remember who was walking the dog. It might have been a man or a woman in a long coat.

'Your mum's made a complaint and Social Services has a duty to investigate it.'

Mum doesn't think I should be living in Cranley Crescent. Rose says she has offered to provide me with a temporary living situation until things have been sorted out. Rose says it doesn't mean that I won't be able to go back to my flat eventually. Rose says she knows it's not ideal but I mustn't panic. She won't give up on me. But she has to follow rules. She has to go through the process. It might take some time. It's only temporary.

'When can I go home?'

'Marilyn, do you understand what I have just said?'

I want to see Gail. I want to hear about Jenny and Jake and Greg.

7

Gail brought me in Jake's old walkman to wear so I can listen to music and not be bored. She's also lending me some of her tapes but she doesn't have any of Marilyn Monroe. Mine are at home because I didn't pack a bag before I came here. The gold collection has two tapes and all the songs from her films. My favourite songs are, *'I Wanna be Loved by You'* and *'Diamonds are a Girl's Best Friend.'*

Jake doesn't use the walkman any more because now he uses an iPod which Gail says is better than a walkman and is what all the youngsters use nowadays. Gail laughs when she talks about Jake. I wish I had a mum like Gail. I love Mum because she is my mum but she's not like Gail. Gail says that she's going to look out for more Marilyn Monroe stuff for me now that she knows about my collection. She says that you can get all sorts of stuff from the internet.

I ask Gail how you get things off the internet. Gail says that you have to be careful about shopping online but I don't think I could do it anyway because I don't have any bank cards, only a Post Office account that my benefit gets paid into. Mum says that money is very important because the people with the money have all the power and the people like us are nothing. If Jake is a footballer, he might earn lots of money like David Beckham. Mum says that if she could have her life over again, she would do it all different. She would have tried harder at school instead of leaving when she was fourteen and she would have made something of herself. Gail made something of herself. She made herself a nurse. She would like Jake to make himself a doctor. I don't think I am nothing even if I am not something.

'Gail?'

'Yes, Poppet?'

'How many bedrooms have you got in your house?'

'How many rooms? Gosh, let's see. Three, sort of, four.'

Gail scratches her nose like she is thinking hard. Her hair's a bit greasy today. Mine is getting greasy again too.

'How can you have sort of a room?'

'Well, we have a spare room which…'

'Is it spare?' Gail has a spare room. Maybe, I could stay in Gail's spare room and not go to Mum and Steve's.

'Well, it's supposed to be a study for the children and it has a sofa bed for when my mum comes to stay.'

Gail has a mum. I have told Gail lots of things about my mum but she hasn't told me anything about hers. Even mums have mums. But not Mum because her mum is dead and she didn't have a dad like me.

'Do you like your mum?'

Gail frowns and shifts from one foot to the other like Penny does. When I go home, after I've stayed at Gail's, I can have Penny and Gillian round for a cup of tea.

'I like, I love my mum,' she says. She rolls her eyes. 'But it's not always easy with mums, is it, Poppet? She doesn't always approve.'

I like Gail telling me about her mum. I think it might mean we are friends. Gail looks tired today. The skin under her eyes is grey. Gail looks after all these people but she needs someone to look after her. I could look after Gail.

'Does she stay there a lot?'

'Too much!' She laughs.

'Would you like it if she didn't come too much?'

'Oh, I suppose so. Anyway, I must get on.' Gail stands up straight and smoothes down her dress even though there are no creases. It is very stiff like card. Nurses' uniforms are not like normal clothes.

'I could stay in the room if you like and then she wouldn't have to stay there.'

'Oh, Poppet.' Gail looks sad.

'I would pay you rent because I get housing benefit to pay rent at Cranley Crescent but I don't know how you swap it over to a new house. I can ask Rose. Rose will tell us what to do.'

'Marilyn…' Gail sits on the edge of the bed.

'We get on very well, don't we? You're my friend, aren't you?'

'Marilyn, I think you're a lovely girl but you can't stay in my house, Poppet.' She smiles but it's not a happy smile, it's a sad smile. I've seen lots of people smile sad smiles at the day centre. Like when Sharon told us that Ben had to move away because he couldn't cope. Cope means that you can do things yourself and you don't cry every day. I can cope. I only cry some days. I cry if people are horrible to me or something bad happens. That's allowed.

'But why?'

'Because my house is full.' She's still smiling the sad smile. 'And because I'm your nurse and you're my patient. And because your mum is going to take care of you for a while.'

Mum didn't want me then she did then she didn't then she did. If I had a baby, I would love it and never give it away. Joan had a baby, once, but they didn't think she'd be able to look after a baby, so she had to go to a special clinic and she told me that they did something to kill it and she saw it slide out of her. She'll never forget. She was screaming and screaming and they had to give her an injection to calm her down. She told me it can't happen again because they did something else to make sure.

'I know mums aren't always easy to get along with, Marilyn. But your mum wants to do what's right by you. She loves you.'

'Gail?'

'Yes, Poppet?'

'Can you help me write a letter?'

'Well, okay. I should really get on with my rounds but, well…'

Gail gets some paper and an envelope. I tell her I don't want anyone else to open it so she says we can write, 'To be opened by addressee only' on the envelope and that will stop anyone like Keith's mum or dad opening it. But Gail says that they can actually still open it if they want to so we better not write anything that is too private. This makes me cross but Gail is only trying to help so I say, 'Okay'.

8

Marilyn Monroe's birthday is 1st June and it is marked on my calendar at home and my calendar here with the white cat. My birthday is also in June but not on the 1st. My birthday is 29th. This is four weeks after Marilyn Monroe's so we are close together. I know this is right even if I'm not that good at dates because I worked it out on the calendar. Rose says that dates are very important so you should mark them down in a diary or a calendar. I have a pink diary and a Marilyn Monroe calendar but it is best just to use one because otherwise you can get confused if you put some dates in the diary and others in the calendar and you might forget something important so I just use the calendar.

The most important date is your birthday because that is when you were born so it is important to celebrate it even if you just buy a cake for yourself or go out for a pizza with your friends. I buy a cake on Marilyn Monroe's birthday too and I light a candle in her memory like Elton John's song, '*Candle in The Wind*', which he wrote for Marilyn Monroe. I hope someone sings a song for me on my birthday after I am dead. Natasha used to worry about me lighting candles in the flat when I was on my own because she thought I might burn the house down or burn myself like a kebab. She made me promise that I would only light candles when she was there or Rose or Sharon or Mum or someone else like that. I promised but it was only pretend because I had my fingers crossed behind my back so it doesn't count.

I love lighting candles. I have lots and lots of candles in all different colours. I keep on buying them: tall long candles and short fat candles; round or square; proper candles and tea lights; ones that smell and ones that don't; red, brown, blue, green, gold, white and lavender. I like burning lavender candles in the bathroom or bedroom. When you light them, the whole room smells of lavender. You can get other smells as well, like frankincense and myrrh for Christmas. I buy lots of cigarette lighters as well because they are a bit safer than matches and it's better to be safe than sorry.

Marilyn Monroe has got a different star sign from me. She is Gemini and I am Cancer. I should be Gemini really because it means twins and I was a twin before Janey died. Marilyn Monroe wasn't a twin ever. Natasha used to read the stars for me out of the paper. I like reading horoscopes but only when they say good things are going to happen. I don't like it when it says things like, 'this is going to be a tough week' or 'loved ones will test your patience on Wednesday' because then I worry about what it means and whether Keith is going to stop being my boyfriend. I asked Gail to read me my horoscope this morning. It said, 'Today, you might end up feeling like you're on a roller coaster ride.' I don't know if that's good or bad because rides are supposed to be fun like when we went to a day trip to Alton Towers with the day centre. But I threw up afterwards, which wasn't so fun and I felt sick for the rest of the day.

I feel sick today.

I should be Gemini and Marilyn Monroe should be Cancer. Cancer people are very sensitive and emotional. Marilyn Monroe was very sensitive and emotional and she used to get upset and cry lots of the time. People said she didn't cope well and she drank lots and took pills and things. I don't drink lots only sometimes like parties. Sometimes I take sleeping pills but not for a long time. I do believe the stars but I don't like the word cancer because it makes me think of the other cancer when you get ill and maybe die or maybe have all your hair fall out because of the chemicals they pump through your body like happened to Mum's friend, Anne.

Other dates that you should mark on your calendar or diary are when your period is due (and you must tell someone when it is late), your Care Planning Meetings, doctor's appointments and days when people are visiting (like Natasha because sometimes I used to forget and go out when she was coming), other people's birthdays (so you don't forget to buy them a card or present if you really like them) and Christmas and New Year (but I missed those). You can also buy an advent calendar specially for Christmas when you get to open one window every day and eat a chocolate, which is fun.

Today is a very important date.

I feel sick like I have eaten too much chocolate but I haven't eaten any because you don't get chocolate in hospital, only from visitors if they bring it as a present. I wish Keith came to see me but he didn't. Joan and Paul came and they brought me some grapes. Grapes are quite nice but not as nice as chocolate. I don't know if Keith's mum or dad opened the letter or not. I don't know if he wanted to see me or not. I don't know if he is still my boyfriend or not. He hasn't written me a letter.

Today is 7th January.

'Poppet, your mum's here.'

Gail is smiling her sad smile and pretending to be happy. I can't stay in Gail's spare room because it's not spare. Gail's mum needs it and anyway, Gail isn't my friend. She's just my nurse. Friends can't be nurses or Care Managers. Friends can be people from the day centre (but not the staff) or neighbours (but only really ones who live in Cranley Crescent) or some other people who are like me. Like Keith but he is not my friend because he's my boyfriend or he was my boyfriend but I don't think he is anymore.

I think Natasha could be my friend if she wasn't my support worker. One time, when Natasha was in my flat helping me do cooking, she started crying. Care Managers and nurses and other people who are staff don't do that. She wasn't even chopping onions so it wasn't that. She was helping me bake a cake for Marilyn Monroe's birthday and there aren't any ingredients in cakes that make you cry. When I asked why she was crying, she said that she always cried on birthdays. She said it made her think of her sister, Katie, who she doesn't see much anymore. Your birthday is the most important date because that is when you were born so you should celebrate birthdays.

'Marilyn? We need to get your stuff together now, Poppet.'

Birthdays are supposed to be happy times, aren't they? But you don't always feel happy on your birthday or on someone else's birthday. My birthday is a happy day because it is the day I was born but it is a sad day too because it is the day Janey died. Natasha's sister has something wrong with her too. Rose says we're not supposed to say that we have something wrong with us. We're supposed to say, 'I have a learning disability' but it means the same thing really. And other people will say you are handicapped anyway, like the newspaper. I liked Natasha but sometimes she made me feel a bit scared because she wasn't in charge like Rose or Sharon or Mum or even Gail.

'Marilyn?'

Don't Bother to Knock

9

I didn't get my hair done at Chrissie's but Mum is doing my roots for me with a packet mix.

'Hold still, Jane. Oh, I love this one, don't you, Jane? Holiday! Oh yeah, oh yeah…'

She's got rubber gloves on and we are singing to her Madonna CD, while she squeezes the dye in my roots. She doesn't do it like Chrissie does. Chrissie uses a tub and a special brush but Mum squeezes it out of a tube. It's like she's icing a cake! But it's a horrible smell not like cakes. Mum says it's the peroxide. That means bleach but it's okay. It's different from bleach that you put down the toilet. You have to be careful with household bleach because if you get it on your skin, it will burn you and if you swallow it, you might die. Mum thinks I'm scared of the hair bleach but I know all about it. Chrissie told me at the hairdressers.

Mum has put the tube down and started dancing to Madonna. I would like to get my own CDs but it's okay because I can listen to them when I go home.

'You're gonna look gorgeous when we finish with you, aren't you? Absolutely fucking gorgeous. Just like your mum. Holiday…'

Mum is very happy today. I think she likes me being here even though she won't call me Marilyn. Rose says it is only temporary. Then I can go home to my own flat and I can go to get my hair done properly at Chrissie's. But Mum is being nice to me, so it's okay.

Mum chucks the tube into the sink and wraps my head up in foil, like a turkey.

'Look at you! You look like an alien!'

'No, I don't.'

'Oh, don't look so serious, Jane. It's only a joke.'

'I don't look like an alien. I look like a turkey.'

Mum bursts out laughing and she bends over and holds

herself.

'You're so f-funny. Such a f-fun-ny gir--ll.'

She looks like she's going to wet herself. That makes me laugh. We're laughing so much that snot comes out of my nose.

'Jane!' Mum makes a noise like a pig and starts laughing again.

It is making her cry, she is laughing so much. Her make-up has gone all streaky and she looks funny. Mum can be very funny and very nice sometimes. Like yesterday, she made me a really nice cup of hot chocolate and she let me wear her favourite fluffy white dressing gown because it was so cold. I was hoping it would snow but it didn't. Mummy Barbara used to build snowmen with me in the garden. She let me put a carrot in the head for a nose and two buttons for eyes and we put Daddy Mike's scarf round the snowman. When we were building the snowman, I put my head back and I ate the snow. Sometimes snow feels hot and it can burn you. Sometimes I get mixed up with hot and cold, like when I am running a bath. One time I thought the water felt very hot and then I stepped in and it was ice cold and gave me a shock. Mum told me to be more careful but I can't help it if I feel things wrong.

Sometimes, when I think about it, I pretend that it was Mum who made the snowman with me, not Mummy Barbara. I do that quite a lot. Pretending is also making up stories or it can be called acting. It's what Marilyn Monroe did with her life. She pretended to be lots of different people. In every film, she was a different person. I think that might get confusing having to be different people all the time. Like you might forget which person you really are. Sometimes I forget which Mummy I did things with so I pretend that everything was with Mum and it makes me feel happy.

Mum pulls off some toilet roll and wipes my nose. I stop laughing.

I am not a baby.

I am an adult and I can look after myself.

'I can do that,' I say and take the paper.

'Alright, alright. No need to snatch.'

We hear the door slam and we look at each other's eyes. Mum's eyes are still wet from laughing. She wipes them with toilet roll.

'Ange! I'm home.'

Mum looks at her watch and her face looks worried. When she is worried, her forehead creases up and her eyes look different.

'Alright, love,' Mum calls down the stairs to Steve. 'I'm just doing Jane's hair.'

'Oh, right. What's for tea?'

Steve calls dinner tea. I think that's funny because tea is tea that you drink.

Mum starts talking quietly to me, not loud so Steve can't hear.

'Shit! I should have started the dinner ages ago.'

Then she goes out of the bathroom and shouts down, 'I'm just about to pop something on, love. D'you fancy anything special?'

Steve starts swearing and Mum runs downstairs. After a long time or a short time, the door slams and Mum comes back. I think it might be a long time, because my head is itching and it hurts. Mum's eyes are still wet.

'Right,' she says, with her sad smile. 'Better wash that lot off.'

'Where's Steve?' I ask.

'Oh don't mind him. He's gone to the pub for a bit. He'll be back for dinner.'

Mum washes off the peroxide but it has made my scalp red and when she dries my hair for me, my roots are a different colour to the rest of my hair and it looks stupid.

10

'What the fuck is she screaming for now?'

Steve is cross. Steve is always cross.

People shouldn't come into other people's bedrooms without knocking. People shouldn't come into the bathroom, to have a pee, when someone else is in the bath. Sharon says this is called privacy and it means that people are supposed to knock on the door and not come in unless you say they can. I can hear Mum's feet coming up the stairs very fast. I think she is cross too but I'm not sure if she's cross with me or with Steve. She is asking Steve what the hell is going on. She is asking him to show some respect. Sharon says respecting other people is very important.

'Jesus fucking Christ! Don't look at me like that, Ange. What am I supposed to do if she insists on staying in the bath all fucking day, eh? Drag her out so I can take a piss? Eh? Is that what you want me to do?'

Steve zips up his jeans and flushes the toilet. He leaves the toilet seat up and it smells bad. I'm not allowed to light any lavender candles in Mum's bathroom but at least she has a bath and not just a shower with a plastic seat so I can lay in the water for a long time. I like having baths.

'Jane. Get out of that bath and get dressed.'

Mum has her arms crossed. Mum is cross.

'But Mum…'

'You do as I say while you are living under my roof.'

Mum is cross with me so I do what she says but my towel is wet because I pulled it in the bath when Steve came in.

'Wait until Steve's left the room, for heaven's sake, Child!'

I am not a child. I am an adult.

Mum rolls her eyes. I can see Steve's face in the mirror. I don't like the face that Steve pulls. Steve scratches his head and I see white flakes fall out of his head. It is called dandruff. You can get special shampoos to get rid of it called

Head and Shoulders. Penny and Gillian have it in their bathroom cabinet. Penny has lots of dandruff and her hair is black. Dandruff looks worse if your hair is black because you can see it more. Steve's hair is brown like mud or stones.

Mum shuts the door behind Steve. She still has her arms crossed and her eyes are moving around a lot.

'Men,' she says and sighs as she puts down the toilet seat and sits on it. She passes me another towel. She is watching me.

Nearly all the colours on my body are gone now. I can't see any purple or blue or red. There is still a little bit of yellow but that's okay because yellow is a happy colour. It is the colour of blonde hair like Marilyn Monroe's and mine. It is the colour of bananas and the sun and sand. It makes me think of eating banana sandwiches on the beach with Keith even though the beach in Southend is made of pebbles and not much sand. I mustn't think about Keith anymore. I must get a new boyfriend. But I will wait until I get back to Southend because if I get a boyfriend in Dagenham, it will be no good when I go home to Cranley Crescent.

'Mum, can I go out?'

Mum is not watching me anymore. She is staring out of the window, through the blinds. This is no yellow sun today. It is grey and raining.

'Mum?'

'What, love?'

'Can I go out?'

Mum looks tired. She hasn't got her red lipstick on today and her hair is all messy.

'Where do you want to go?'

'Anywhere.'

She watches me again. I have got the new towel wrapped around me tight. She looks at the top of the towel where my chest is squashed. Sometimes Steve looks there too. Like Keith's dad who looks at bras.

She slaps her jeans and says, 'You can come with me to the

53

Post Office if you want.'

Going to the Post Office doesn't sound like much fun but it's better than staying here with Steve. I don't like it when Mum goes out and leaves me alone with Steve. He gives me the creeps. I don't know if he fancies me or not. He shouldn't fancy me because he is Mum's boyfriend but sometimes he looks at me like he fancies me. Other times, he looks at me like he hates me. He never looks at me just normal.

Mum stands up.

'Yes. Let's go to the Post Office, Jane. Keep you out of trouble, eh? Snap snap. Get dressed, Jane. Let me put my face on.'

She leaves me to get ready. I can hear her arguing with Steve downstairs. I hear Steve's voice shouting, 'she', 'her' and 'your daughter'. I hear Mum's voice keep saying, 'Jane'. My name is Marilyn. I put on a pair of Mum's jeans. Rose said she can get some of my clothes for me and bring them when she visits but Mum said it was better to leave them there. She said I don't need all those little dresses, do I? She said it's probably better for someone like me not to wear those clothes. But she doesn't know that I am going to keep on wearing them as soon as I am allowed back to Cranley Crescent.

I look in the mirror. I don't think my face is so bad now but Mum says I have to go back to see the doctor another day. I'm not sure what day that is because I think I missed some days off the calendar and now I don't know what day it is. I don't want to ask Mum what day it is because then she'll look at me like I'm stupid and Steve will say something like I told you she was stupid and they might start talking about putting me in a home again and I am not going to live in a home. I would rather kill myself. Some people say Marilyn Monroe killed herself and some people say that's a lie.

I put on blue eyeliner to go out to the Post Office because it's important to make the most of yourself. I stretch the skin of my eyelid to keep it steady like Sharon showed me. Then I draw round the top, from lash to lash. It's a bit like doing a dot-to-dot picture! Some people at the day centre like John and Susan who live in a home still do dot-to-dots and jigsaw puzzles. I'm in the singing group and do dancing and hair and make-up. I don't do puzzles. Natasha used to do her makeup at my house sometimes, if she was going out afterwards. She didn't teach me how to do it like Sharon, but I used to watch how she did hers. She looks very different with her makeup on because she looks very young without it. She does her eyes very black to match her hair and clothes. Mum says Natasha is a punk. I think that's why she doesn't like her.

Mum is coming back up the stairs.

My eye is watering because I pressed a bit too hard when Steve started shouting again.

'Jane?'

She comes in without knocking too. But it's okay because I am dressed and because she is my mum so she is allowed even though I still don't like it. She smells of Charlie Red now and she has her red lipstick on.

'Jane!'

It's all smudged now because of my eye watering.

'You don't need to put all that muck on!'

Mum has green eyeshadow on her eyelids and black eyeliner all the way round her eyes. It isn't even on that well. I can see some smudges on the corners. Maybe she pressed to hard too or maybe Steve made her cry. I think she cries a lot. More than me.

'You have.'

'Less of the cheek, please,' says Mum and I think she might shout but then she laughs. 'Oh, go on, then. Come here, let me do it for you.'

I don't want her to do it for me because I am an adult not a baby and Rose says I can do things for myself. But I don't want to make Mum cross again so I let her do it. I think she would like it if I was still a child but not a baby because she

55

gave me away when I was a baby. If I had a baby, I would love it and never give it away. Marilyn Monroe wanted a baby so much that it made her go a bit crazy because she was so sad that she didn't have one. I think Mum liked me best when I was nine and she thought I was funny.

11

I don't know what day it is because Steve tore up my calendar in a fight but it feels like I've been here a very long time. Tonight, we are having fish and chips. Mum and me are going to get it from the fish shop that we used to go to when I was nine. It still has the orange sun painted on the window but different people work there now. They are Chinese people and they have a different New Year from us. They sell Chinese food like spring rolls, as well as fish and chips. The man who works here told us last week that they were celebrating the New Year. I told Steve and he tore up my calendar. He doesn't like Chinese people. He doesn't like many people.

'Come on, Jane.'

Mum is holding my hand to cross the road. I don't like this but I let her do it. I imagine that I am holding Janey's hand.

Mum tells me to sit on the chair while she gets in the queue. I can smell chips with salt and vinegar and it makes my mouth water. The man behind the counter is wrapping up a bag of chips for the woman at the front of the queue. He leaves the bag open and she shakes salt and vinegar on top. Then she squirts on ketchup. He smiles at me and Mum turns round and gives me a nasty look. I chew on my roll-neck because I am hungry and because I don't know what else to do and I shouldn't look at men when I'm out in public because they might get the wrong idea about me.

Roll-necks are good in the cold because they keep you warm. Mum bought me this black roll-neck jumper and some other jumpers in dark green, blue and grey. They are not very nice colours. I wanted pink, orange and red but Mum said these colours are best because they don't attract attention or give the wrong idea. The roll-necks are nice and high because it is important to keep yourself covered up. But they make my neck itch and I saw lots of red bumps on my neck when I looked in the bathroom mirror. The doctor says that the scars are healing very nicely. Much better than he would have dared imagine. I'm a very lucky girl. He smiles at me too. You have to be careful about men smiling at you.

I think people got the wrong idea about Marilyn Monroe a lot of times. She didn't wear roll-neck jumpers much. She wore a lot of dresses that showed too much. That's what Mum says. Mum says how can anyone expect to be taken seriously, if they dress like a whore? Women who dress like whores are asking for it. Mum used to wear dresses but now she wears roll-necks like me. Steve tells Mum what to wear and she tells me what to wear. I tell Janey what to wear. She can wear pretty dresses with lots of pink flowers on. She can have her hair in curls. She smiles at me too but that's okay because she's just a child.

'Three plaice and chips,' says the man behind the counter, as he gives Mum the food.

I don't look up because I mustn't give the man the wrong idea.

'Come on, Jane,' says Mum.

'Will Steve be out at the pub?'

I hope Steve is at the pub because then it will just be me and Mum and we might have a laugh together again. We never laugh together when Steve is there.

'Don't be silly, Jane. We're all having tea together tonight, for once, aren't we? Like a proper family.'

'Oh yeah.'

We're all having tea together like a proper family but I don't think we are a proper family. A proper family is a husband and a wife who have a baby and keep it and then they might have another baby that is a sister or a brother. My mum gave me away when I was a baby. If I had a baby, I would love it and never give it away. Steve is not my family. Janey is my family. I will be with her, not Steve. Marilyn had a half sister. Half sister is a funny word. It means that you don't have the same mum or you don't have the same dad, not that you are half a sister. You can't really be a half because then you wouldn't be a person. But some people are born joined together so they might share a body. They are called Siamese Twins. There was a picture in Mum's magazine of two girls who shared half a body.

Janey and me weren't Siamese twins. We had a whole body each. One for her and one for me. Her body died. Some people say that when your body dies it is the end and some people say that it isn't the end. I can't imagine the end because then what would you see? You wouldn't see anything because you wouldn't have any eyes. Some people say that your soul goes to heaven or into a new body or you become a ghost. Janey's body died but I don't know about her soul. I've been thinking about Janey a lot since I came to Mum's. I keep seeing her and she makes me feel happy. I don't know if she is a ghost or if she is inside my head or if she is just there.

'Jane!' Mum is shouting. A car is beeping. Janey laughs and runs away in her flowery dress. 'Look where you're going for Christ sakes!'

Steve is sitting in front of the TV, watching football. I don't like football because it is so boring. It is lots of men kicking one ball. They should have more balls because then it wouldn't take so long to get them in the net. Steve is sitting on the edge of the sofa, not lying down like usual. He is moving up and down like he is about to jump up. I don't like the way he's doing this. I don't think Mum likes it either because her face looks screwed up. She is holding a tray with Steve's fish and chips on it. She has taken the fish and chips out of the paper and put it on a nice plate with blue lines round the edge. There is a can of lager on the tray too, even though he's got one in his hand. I am holding the tray with my dinner on it and I am standing next to Mum because I don't want to sit down next to Steve on the sofa.

Steve is ignoring her and watching the TV. Mum said we

were all having tea together like a proper family. I hate Steve. Janey comes up behind me and holds onto my leg. I look at the table at the other side of the room and wonder if Mum will get cross if I take my tray over there.

'Steve, love. The dinner's ready. Are you going to…'

'GOAL!' he shouts and jumps up and the tray with his dinner on it goes up in the air and chips go up in the air and land on the floor and the fish falls in the sofa and breaks in two and the can of lager falls off and hits me on the foot and I'm not wearing the slippers that Mum told me to and my foot hurts.

The lager doesn't spill anywhere because it isn't opened yet. So Mum won't have to clean lager off the floor.

I am still holding my tray.

Janey is scared. I tell her not to be scared.

Steve makes his eyes very big and points them at me. Not Mum or the tray or the fish on the sofa or the chips or the lager on the floor.

'What the fuck is she doing now? Talking to herself?'

'I'm sorry. I'm sorry. I'm sorry. I'm sorry…' Mum keeps saying it and then she gets down on her hands and knees and puts everything on the tray.

'Stop fucking looking at me, you mong!'

Janey starts crying.

I take my tray to the table.

Mum takes the tray out to the kitchen then she brings back another one and gives it to Steve. Steve eats the fish and chips that was supposed to be Mum's dinner.

I give my chips to Janey to stop her crying.

12

Marilyn Monroe loved animals. Once, she asked Jimmy if she could bring a cow into the house so it didn't have to stand in the rain. Everyone thought this was funny and stupid but I think it was kind because cows can't hold umbrellas to keep dry. They need people to look after them. Some people think that disabled people can't look after themselves either but Rose says they say that because they don't understand. It is called ignorance. Rose says I am an adult and I can make my own decisions and I can look after myself but I just need a bit of support. You can get support from family and friends or support workers who get paid to support you. Natasha is a support worker.

No pets are allowed in Cranley Crescent. It's one of the rules. It is called an agreement and if you break the rules, it means they can make you leave your flat. Other rules are no smoking and no painting walls or putting up shelves without asking. You are allowed to paint your walls and put up shelves if you ask first but they don't want you to do any damage. Some people don't keep to the rules. Like Joan and Paul drilled a hole in the bathroom wall to hang up a mirror but it went wrong and Rose was very cross and made them have an urgent Review Meeting but didn't make them leave the flat. Penny and Gillian have got gerbils who run around on wheels all day and no-one has told them that they have to leave. I painted my bedroom wall pink but I asked first and Natasha helped me do it. It's called shocking pink and it is very bright. Natasha got shocking pink paint in her black hair and she laughed and said it looked cool and she left it in for two days before she washed it out.

Natasha hasn't seen her sister, Katie for two years. I think two years is a long time because it is two birthdays and two Christmases. I don't know why she hasn't seen her. I think it might be because Katie is disabled but that would be a very bad reason. If that was the reason, I don't know why Natasha was helping me. I would like to meet Katie and see if she looks like Natasha. I told Mum about Katie. Mum says its disgusting that Natasha can't even look after her own flesh and blood. She says that people like that shouldn't be able to look after other people's children. But I am not a child. I am an adult and I can make my own choices. She says it must be the guilt. She says Natasha is fucked up in the head and she's not coming anywhere near me again.

Some sisters don't see a lot of each other. I think maybe Natasha would like me to be her sister. I would like it too but I would like her to visit Katie and take me with her. Marilyn Monroe didn't see a lot of her half sister. Some sisters aren't good friends like some mums and daughters aren't good friends. I see a lot of Janey now because she lives in Mum's house with me. She sleeps in my bed at night and nobody knows. Just her and me. She didn't come to see me when I lived at Cranley Crescent but I'm going to ask her if she will come and see me when I move back there. I like looking after Janey. I tuck her in bed every night and sing her a lullaby in my head or sometimes out loud but only quiet so that Steve won't come in and tell me to shut the fuck up.

When I get back home to Cranley Crescent, I'm going to ask if I can paint the bathroom walls bright blue to match the blue bath. Marilyn Monroe had all white walls in her house but I like colours. White walls are for hospitals. White is for clean teeth and snow and paper that no-one has written on. Keith never wrote back to my letter. White is for the white trainers of boys who attack girls at bus stops. White is for the moon at night when you can't sleep.

I can't sleep tonight. I can hear Mum and Steve making noises next door. I don't know if they are fighting or having sex. I don't know if I will ever have sex again.

13

I'm sitting on Mum's lap and she's brushing my hair with a purple brush. She bought it from the pound shop in the high road, last time we went shopping. All the food is nearly gone. I don't know when we can get more money from the Post Office. Steve is at the pub, which is good, except when he comes home again.

'Baby Jane,' whispers Mum. 'My little baby Jane. Why don't I give you a bath? Would you like that, my little baby Jane?'

Mum is brushing my hair a bit too hard, so it hurts. I think she's been drinking too much. She is holding a bottle and drinking out of the top. There is a bottle next to me on the sofa. I have seen empty bottles on the floor and in the sink and on the table and on the sofa. The glass is different colours. Some are clear, some are yellow, some are green and some are brown. They are like people but people aren't green. They are all different shapes and sizes. Lots and lots of bottles. They are next to Steve's empty cans, which are squashed up. Sometimes I put them in the bin when no-one is looking.

I am curled up on Mum's lap like a cat but I'm not smelly like a cat because I have a bath every day. It's important to keep yourself clean and have a bath and change your clothes every day. I don't think Mum has changed her clothes today. She smells funny like a custard pie that has gone bad, like the one in the fridge that I threw out when she was asleep on the sofa. She isn't using Charlie Red anymore. Mum is sleeping a lot on the sofa. She sleeps in the day and the afternoon and sometimes the night. It is hard to work out the time. Sometimes we eat coco-pops in the afternoon when *Trisha* is on. I cover Mum up with the blanket or she covers me up. We take turns.

'Come on, baby Jane,' says Mum and she tries to pick me

up and carry me but I am too heavy, so I put my arms around her and curl my body round her to make myself small like a baby. Like her little baby Jane. Mum has started singing lullabies to me again, like I sing to Janey. It makes Janey feel safe, so she can go to sleep and have nice dreams instead of nightmares. Mum heard me singing to Janey and she came into my room and sat on the bed and started singing it with me.

'Go to sleep my baby, close your pretty eyes, go to sleep my baby, dream of parrot's eyes.'

She laughed and said I was her funny girl. Funny, funny baby Jane.

We've been having our dinner without Steve. Just the two of us. Just the two of us, Mummy and baby Jane. Steve comes home late. Mum says it's important that I go to my room before he comes home. I must remember to keep the bathroom door locked and not to have baths when he is here. Yesterday, we had pie and chips from the shop and Mum cut up my pie for me. Then we had pink raspberry jelly and ice-cream because it's my favourite and Mum fed me with a spoon. It was a special treat but we can't have it every day because we're not made of money.

There are lots of bubbles in the bath and a rubber duck. Mum bought a non-slip mat and put it in the bath. She saw it in Mrs. Tulser's bath and it's a good idea for frail people who might slip over and hurt themselves. Mum said it was a good idea for me to have one too. Mum says I'm a very lucky girl to have a mum who takes such good care of her. If I am a very good girl, I can stay here and I won't have to go into a home like Mrs. Tulser. Mrs. Tulser smiled at me when we visited. It's okay to smile at an old lady but you mustn't smile at men or they get the wrong idea. Mrs. Tulser smelt like bad custard too and she wet herself when we were there because I saw the wet patch on the bed when she got up and it smelt like fish. Mrs. Tulser started crying and she called me, 'Lily'. I don't know who Lily is.

Mum says Steve isn't a bad man, not really. He just loses control sometimes. He can't help the way he is. It's the drink. He can't help it. She says it's not his fault. Some people have problems. We all have our problems. That's what she says. Mum says he doesn't mean to hurt her. He loves her very much. He's just a man. Just like all the rest. Probably out with a bit of skirt again. But he's sorry, really sorry. He promised he won't do it again.

Mum is soaping up my back and her nails are sharp. They dig in my back. I can see red lines on my arms from her nails. Clean, clean, all clean. She looks at her watch. Time is getting on. We better hurry up. Mum will be getting Steve's dinner ready soon. Time for bed soon. Don't pull out the plug. Mummy will use the water. Mummy is wrapping up baby Jane and putting her to bed now. Goodnight, baby Jane. Mummy loves you very much.

Love Happy

14

My new boyfriend is called Wesley. He is very nice and he is going to take me out later when he gets back from college. He is learning mechanics and he can drive a car. He is better than Keith. He is one year older than me. I met him two days ago, outside the fish and chip shop. I was coming out with fish and chips for me and Mum and he was going in to get a Chinese takeaway. His favourite is spare ribs and special fried rice and he drinks Dr Pepper. I go to the fish and chip shop by myself now because Mum is sleeping all the time. Mum and me got some money from the Post Office and I take it out of her purse and go and buy the dinner every day.

I smile at the man behind the counter because Mum isn't watching. He asks me how Mum is and I tell him that she's not feeling well. He tells me that he has a daughter called Mai about my age and she is away studying at university. I ask him what it is like and he says he doesn't know. He says it's like a big school where you learn. I thought that was called a college like where Wesley goes. I would like to go to college and do learning. He says Mai's learning to be a doctor and that will make him very happy. It makes me think of Gail. Gail wants Jake to be a doctor. I wouldn't like to be a doctor because you'd have to see people's guts hanging out. I would like to learn hairdressing. I learnt some things at the day centre like how to look after your hair and do plaits but I want to go to a proper college now, like Wesley and Mai. I want to get a job so I don't have to wait for the Post Office to give me money, so I can buy what I want with my money, like a new lipstick or a car. I would like to learn how to drive. I think I'm going to ask Wesley to teach me.

Sometimes I sit in the fish and chip shop and talk to the Chinese man behind the counter whose daughter is Mai because it's boring staying at home while Mum sleeps and it smells bad in the house now, even though I try to keep it clean and tidy. It's important to keep your house clean and hygienic. Sharon taught me about hygiene in the home. You have to be careful with household bleach because if you get it on your skin, it will burn you and if you swallow it, you might die. I haven't seen Sharon for a long time or Natasha. Sometimes Sharon and Natasha told me different things, like Natasha didn't believe in bleach. She bought special cleaning things from the health food shop because she said they were kind to the planet but I don't know what that means. She said I shouldn't believe everything they tell me at the day centre. I can make my own mind up.

Sometimes the Chinese man behind the counter gives me a free spring roll or bag of chips for lunch. Wesley said he'd been watching me sitting there from the launderette across the road. He said he thought I looked nice and he wished I could sit and talk to him instead. I will sit and talk to anyone who is nice. I like being friendly to people. Sharon says it's called being sociable. I haven't seen Sharon for a long time. Mum doesn't like me being sociable. Marilyn Monroe was sociable. I bet she had lots of friends. I miss my friends from Cranley Cresent. I want to talk to my best friend, Joan but I can't remember her phone number.

'What you having today, Marilyn?' asks the man behind the counter.

'Nothing today because I am going out with my boyfriend.'

'Won't Mum mind?'

'No. She'll be sleeping. I'll make her some *Coco Pops* when I get back.'

I don't use the phone very often because when I lived at Cranley Cresent, all my friends were there, so we just knocked on each other's houses when we wanted to chat. Joan would come round if she had a fight with Paul and we'd have a cup of tea. Penny and Gillian like to pop in nearly every day. Sometimes, I would go round to Frank's to check if he wanted anything at the shops. If we needed to talk to a member of staff, we pressed a special button on the phone marked with a star and it went straight through to a special mobile phone. You never knew who would answer it. It might be Natasha or Rose or Ryan or someone else. They have to take turns. It is part of their jobs. You could ring it at any time of the night or day. It is called 24 hour on call but you're not supposed to ring after dinner time unless it's an emergency. An emergency is if someone is hurt or you are in danger. An emergency isn't if your kettle is broken or you can't find a matching pillow case.

Once I pressed the star button and it rang but nobody answered it. They promised that somebody would always answer it. I told Rose about that when she came to see me in hospital before. I don't know if I should have told her that. It was the night before the party and I was trying to wash my gold dress in the washing machine and it wouldn't work. It was an emergency because I needed the dress to be clean for the party. When Natasha came the next day, she laughed and said it was just as well the washing machine hadn't worked because the dress was dry clean only and I would have ruined it. She said it was perfectly clean as it was.

'Where are you meeting your boyfriend?' asks the man.

'I'm meeting him here,' I say and the man smiles.

'He is coming to meet me soon.'

'It's like this is your house!' he laughs. He is a nice man. Like my friend, Billy and my boyfriend, Wesley.

I wish I had my gold dress so I could wear it for Wesley. I'm not wearing the roll-neck today. I borrowed a top out of Mum's wardrobe. It is red and it has a scoop neck and I'm wearing it with tight jeans. I borrowed her red lipstick and her Charlie Red perfume even though I don't like it that much. I am sitting looking out of the window so that I can see when Wesley gets here. Wesley lives with his brother. I haven't met his brother, yet. Wesley asked me where I live and I told him that I'm staying with Mum and Steve but it's only for a little while. I told him I've got my own flat in Southend and he said, 'Cool'. I don't want Wesley to meet Mum and Steve.

71

'Why don't you have a spring roll, while you wait?' asks the man. I asked his name before and he keeps telling me but I can't say it right.

'Nah.'

Wesley is coming soon. Wesley says he wished he'd met me before two days ago. But I said at least we found each other now. Sometimes, it can take people a long time to find their real soul mate. Like Marilyn Monroe married the wrong man, first of all. Then she met Arthur at a party and he was her one true love. Parties are good places to meet people but you can meet people anywhere, like in the day centre or the street or a fish and chip shop. A man started talking to me in the post office the other day and asked me if I wanted to go back to his house and suck his cock. I told him to go away. I'm not stupid.

I breathe on the window and watch it steam up. Then I write my name in the steam with my finger. My name is Marilyn. I draw a heart underneath and look through it. I can see Wesley crossing the road and it makes my heart beat really fast. He's smiling. I wave at him. He looks very sexy but we haven't had sex yet. I think he would be good at sex. Better than Keith.

'Bye!' I say to the man behind the counter and I run out the door and put my arms round Wesley's neck. It feels smooth and hot and he smells of cocoa butter.

'Wo! Hello, gorgeous,' says Wesley and he kisses me. He is a very good kisser. I think I would like to have sex with him soon but I want it to be making love.

He holds my hand and we start walking. I look at my white hand in his black hand. Our hands look nice together. His skin isn't really black, it is brown and my skin isn't really white, it's pink. But people say you are black or you are white. Steve doesn't like black people but I don't care because Steve is stupid and I don't like Steve. I am an adult and I can pick my own friends and I can pick my own boyfriends.

Wesley smiles at me and looks at our hands too.

I like it when he holds my hand.

'So where are we going?' I ask him.

He asks if I'm hungry. I tell him yes because I didn't eat any spring rolls. I am sick of spring rolls and chips. I ask to go to McDonalds because I feel like eating a burger and he says he can take me somewhere better than that if I want. I say McDonald's is alright. When we queue up, he still holds my hand and he kisses me on the neck. I love Wesley. I ask him when it's Valentines' Day but he says it's gone. We'll have to wait until next year. He says next Valentines' Day, we'll do something really special.

15

Marilyn Monroe had three husbands. I only want one husband. One true love. Marlin Monroe's first husband was her neighbour, Jimmy. I don't want to marry any of my neighbours. Not the ones here or in Cranley Crescent. I think marrying Jimmy was probably a mistake. Sharon says everyone makes mistakes. It's okay to make a mistake because you learn from it. Maybe Marilyn Monroe learnt that you shouldn't marry your neighbours. I don't know.

Her second husband was a famous baseball player called Joe and he gave her a wedding ring with thirty-five diamonds on it. I saw it on the TV because it was sold in an auction for nearly a million dollars. I think she must have liked diamonds a lot because she sang that they are a girl's best friend. My best friend is Joan and I miss her but if I go back to Cranley Crescent, I'll miss Wesley but Wesley could come and live with me in my flat like Paul lives with Joan. I want to be married first, though. Not like Joan and Paul.

It must have been really exciting for Marilyn Monroe to marry a famous baseball player, maybe like marrying David Beckham or someone really gorgeous and rich and famous. Posh wore a purple wedding dress when she married Becks but I think you should get married in white. I will get married in white. It must have been very exciting to marry Joe, the baseball player, but I don't think it was true love. They got divorced after a few months but Marilyn Monroe stayed married to Arthur for nearly five years which is quite good.

I think Arthur was Marilyn Monroe's one true love even though they got divorced in the end. Some people love each other too much so it doesn't work out but it doesn't mean they didn't love each other. If you love someone too much, it hurts. You can't eat or sleep or think about anything else. I think maybe this is what happened with Marilyn Monroe and Arthur. They drove each other mad. I can't eat because I love Wesley so much but I won't go mad. Marilyn Monroe was scared about going mad because her mum was in a mental hospital, which is where they lock up mad people.

Marilyn Monroe didn't want to end up in a mental hospital. She didn't want to be locked up and made to stay in bed and not allowed out and not allowed to do anything at all. Like I don't want to end up in a home like Mrs. Tulser. But I might visit her again soon because I don't think Mum has been to see her since we last went and I feel sorry for her left by herself all day to wet the bed and ask for Lily. She must be lonely. I don't know if Lily is married. Lily is the name of a flower. I think lilies are for when people die. I don't want lilies when I get married. I want a hundred yellow roses because roses are for romance and yellow is a happy colour.

'Yo, Wes!' Someone is calling.

We turn round. The man who is calling Wesley is not wearing a happy colour. He is wearing black and blue and purple. It makes me think of Mum's eyes after Steve hits her. He is wearing a black baseball cap but I don't think he is a baseball player like Marilyn Monroe's second husband.

Wesley starts chatting to the man in the black baseball cap. He calls him Zig. I think Zig must be a friend from college. Wesley is talking to Zig in a different way to the way he talks to me. I don't understand what they are saying. I want to go to the toilet but I don't know where it is. I look at Zig while Wesley talks to him. He is white not black or brown like Wesley. But I think he wants to be black. Maybe he likes pretending to be black but you can't pretend your face is black if it is white because they are two different colours. His hair is shaved in zig-zags.

'Is this your bird, man?' says Zig and he starts walking round me in a circle. I don't like the way he is looking at me, looking and laughing.

Wesley tells him my name is Marilyn and Zig makes a noise like a howl.

'She's nasty, man. Nasty.'

75

Wesley looks angry. He is breathing hard.

'Stop it, man. Show some respect.'

But Zig doesn't stop it and I start getting dizzy. He goes round and round and I look down at his trainers. They are blue with white stripes. He goes round and round and the colours blur. I see the boys' white trainers. I'm at the bus stop and they are round me in a circle. They are all talking at the same time and asking me questions, so I don't know who to answer. Where are you going, girlie? Have you got a boyfriend? Are you going to meet your sugar daddy for a fuck? I bet you like it up the arse, don't you? They are all laughing at the same time and making noises that scare me. They are all looking at me at the same time with different coloured eyes. Different coloured skin. Different coloured clothes. So many colours.

Round and round and round.

I think I'm going to be sick.

I feel someone push me.

I scream.

'Stop it, man. I mean it.'

Wesley pushes Zig away.

'Yo, man!' Zig puts his hands up in the air and walks away, shaking is head with his zig-zag hair.

Wesley puts his arm around me.

'You okay?'

I feel very hot.

'I need to go to the toilet.'

Wesley shows me where the toilet is and waits for me outside. Everything is moving round in front of me.

'Are you alright, love?' asks a woman with a baby in a pushchair who is coming out of the toilet.

The baby has curly hair and he is smiling and kicking his legs. I smile at the woman with her baby. They both have chubby cheeks and freckles. She has a baby and loves him and would never give him away. She isn't wearing a wedding ring so she doesn't have a husband but she might have a boyfriend who loves her like crazy like Steve loves Mum.

I go in and sit on the toilet and put my head on my knees to stop things moving. When I wipe myself, there is blood. It is my period. It hurts and I feel hot. My period is heavy. I haven't had normal periods for ages because of the injection. I haven't got any tampons so I have to roll up some toilet paper and stuff it in my knickers.

When I come out of the toilets, Wesley is still standing there. It makes me feel better to see him. Wesley gets the burgers and we sit down on the red plastic chairs. Wesley strokes my back and waits until I feel okay. He doesn't even eat his burger because I'm not eating mine. I can't eat because I feel sick and because I love Wesley too much. I think Wesley might be my one true love. If he is my one true love, we can get married and have a baby.

16

Wesley says I have the most beautiful body he has ever seen. I tell him that I think Marilyn Monroe is the most beautiful woman that ever lived and he says I am his Marilyn Monroe. It makes me very happy when he says this. I am his Marilyn Monroe. We are in Wesley's bed. He has his own room with a double bed. Not like the single bed I have to sleep in at Mum's. He has a navy blue duvet cover. It is a boy's colour. Not like pink, peach, lilac and cream. They are the colours of my duvet covers at Cranley Crescent. When I left, the lilac one was on.

When I first came into Wesley's room, he had posters and calendars of women on the wall. The women weren't wearing many clothes in the pictures just bras and knickers. Some were just wearing thongs. I don't like thongs because they dig up your bum. I don't know who the women were but they looked like Jordan and some of them had really big tits. But he has taken all the pictures down now except for a photo of his grannie, who is his favourite person in the whole world, except me. He says he hasn't got eyes for other women anymore. Only me. His Marilyn Monroe.

Wesley's brother is out at work. His name is Patrick. I have met him once and he is nice like Wesley but more quiet. Wesley says Patrick has never had a girlfriend and he is shy around women. I think this is true because Patrick doesn't like to look me in the eyes. He looks at my hands or my feet. It makes me laugh.

Wesley is naked and I am naked and we are pressed together. He says it is beautiful when we are together. It makes me very happy when he says this. Wesley makes me very happy. Having sex with Wesley is making love because we love each other. Wesley strokes my face and kisses me. I snuggle up to Wesley and kiss him on the neck and he starts wanting to have sex again. So, we do it again. He is on top of me and we look at each other's eyes.

'Marilyn, Marilyn, Marilyn…' he keeps saying my name over and over again. It sounds like a song, like a lullaby, like I sing to Janey but I haven't sung to Janey since I met Wesley. I don't say anything but I listen to the noises he makes. Men like to make noises when they have sex. When I first had sex with Jamie, I thought that he was hurting when he made those noises but he told me it means it feels really good. I think I must be very good at sex because Wesley is making lots of noise.

'Marilyn, Marilyn, I love you, Marilyn.'

We are going to get married and have a baby. If it is a girl, I will call it Janey.

Wesley tells me lots of secret things. Like he told me about his last girlfriend, called Jazz. She was Chinese and her parents didn't know about him. They wouldn't let her go out with someone black because she was supposed to marry a Chinese man. It makes me think of the Chinese man, whose daughter is Mai. Wesley asks me what my parents would say about him being black. I told him that I don't have a dad and I don't talk to Mum about boyfriends. Wesley went quiet then. I think he wants to come to my house. I told him that it's not my house and he can come to my flat when I go back home but he was still quiet and I didn't know what to say.

Mum is asleep on the sofa with all the bottle people when I get back. The house is quiet. There are no noises anywhere. I think Steve must be out because he likes to make a lot of noise. He turns the television up loud and slams doors and shouts. But there are no noises today. I sit down on the end of the sofa and stroke Mum's forehead and she keeps her eyes shut. I don't know if she is asleep or pretending. Mum told Rose that she was going to take me home and look after me but she doesn't look after me anymore. I don't mind because I am an adult so I don't need anyone to look after me. Her eyelashes are wet and stuck together and her hair is wet and

79

stuck to her head.

I go to the kitchen and pull open the fridge door and look inside. I couldn't eat my burger but I am hungry now. There are two beers, one carrot and half a pack of butter, with bread crumbs stuck on the side. I can smell something else is hiding. I pull out the vegetable tray and there is a foil box with some curry left in the bottom. I close it again. I open the breadbin and look at the bread. I count the slices. One, two, three, four, five. There are white and blue dots on the bread. Sharon says that this means it is mouldy and you have to throw it away.

I open all the cupboards, one at a time and I find a tin of baked beans. It has a ring pull top. I get a saucepan and pour them in. I try to light the gas but it doesn't light. I have an electric cooker in my flat at Cranley Crescent. Rose says it is safer. I keep pressing the button and it makes a clicking noise but the gas doesn't turn blue. I put my hand on it to feel it but it is not hot. The gas smell is making my head hurt, so I turn it off. I toast the bread and scrape the blue and white dots off like I have seen Natasha do before. I turn the gas on again and press the button and I blow it like I've seen Natasha do and it pops and lights up really high and nearly touches my face and it scares me.

I get two plates from the side. There is a hair on one of the plates. I take it off and wash the plates because it is important to be clean and hygienic in the kitchen or you might get food poisoning. I go back to the living room and stroke Mum's forehead again and put my finger on her eyelids to see if she opens them but she doesn't. She is like a baby. I pretend she is my baby and I lift up her head and put it in my arms and sing her the parrot's eyes lullaby.

Then I remember the beans so I go back to the kitchen but they are burnt on the bottom of the pan. I turn off the cooker. I put the toast on the plates and put on the butter and spoon off the top beans onto the toast, leaving the burnt ones in the pan. I think that will be okay but there aren't many beans on the toast now. There are lots of beans in the pan. I take the plates to where Mum is.

'Mum?'

She doesn't answer.

She doesn't open her eyes.

'Mum? I've made you some food.'

I put the plates down on the floor and try to open her eyes with my fingers.

'Mum?'

I can see a bit of her eyeball but it is red. She opens her eyelids and her eyeballs move up to the top then she closes her eyelids again.

She opens her lips and it smells bad like the drain before Mum puts bleach down it. She starts to make a croak.

'Jane? Jane?'

She doesn't eat her dinner. So I have one and Janey has one.

17

Wesley took me to the cinema today and Patrick came too. I wanted to see the film with Jennifer Lopez but they wanted to see a different one, so I said alright. I sat next to Wesley and Patrick sat next to Wesley on the other side. Patrick was very shy and he didn't say much but he ate lots of popcorn. Wesley kept laughing at the film but I didn't think it was funny. I thought it was boring. There were lots of men in the film and lots of men in the cinema watching it. It was all about cars and chasing and shooting people. I fell asleep with my head on Wesley's shoulder and I only woke up when it finished.

We are walking back to Wesley's and Patrick's house now and they are talking about the film. I am holding Wesley's hand. We walk past the fish and chip shop with the Chinese people and I wave at the Chinese man behind the counter, with my other hand. We walk past Heathway train station and I squeeze Wesley's hand. A woman is coming out with a baby strapped to her. If I had a baby, I would love it and never give it away. There is a photo booth inside the station where people get photos done for their travel card. If you take them to the Post Office you can get a passport which means you are going to another country. I have never been to another country. The places I have been to are Dagenham, Southend, Romford and Leigh-on-Sea.

'Let's get a picture of the three of us!' I say to Wesley and Patrick.

'Yeah, why not!' says Wesley.

Patrick doesn't say anything.

I like having my picture taken and I like putting all the pictures in albums. I have the ones of Aunt Maggie and me in a special album with a silk cover. One of her holding me, wrapped in a yellow blanket and one when I'm sitting on her knee, with a jumper that's too big. I have some of Mummy

Barbara and me and some of Mummy Lynn and me but I don't have any of Mum and me. Mum has some pictures of me from before when I was plain Jane with mousy brown hair and big glasses. I hate them so they are not in my album. I'm glad I don't have to wear glasses anymore because they look ugly. Sharon says you shouldn't say people look ugly because everyone is beautiful in their own special way. But I don't think that's true.

I have lots of pictures from the day centre. There are lots of the singing group when I bought a disposable camera and Sharon took a picture of everyone with me in it, then Billy took a picture of Sharon and me but he cut our heads off the picture. The one with our heads cut off didn't go in the album. Sharon helped me choose a silver frame to put the best picture of the signing group inside. We found it in Woolworths in the Homeware section. It was a very nice frame, with swirly patterns on it. I put it on top of my television in my flat in Cranley Crescent. I bought two frames and in the other one, I put a picture of Marilyn Monroe on one side and a picture of me on the other. Sharon helped me cut the pictures to the right shape and fit them in the frame so it looks as though we are together, the other Marilyn and me.

Wesley gets in first then pulls me on his lap. I love Wesley.

'Quick, put the money in,' says Wesley, giving me the coins.

I lean forward to put the money in and the blue curtain closes in Patrick's face. I pull it back.

'Patrick! Put your head in!' I say to him.

Flash!

'Patrick!'

Flash!

Patrick puts him head in but his head hits my head.

Flash!

'Sorry, Marliyn, I, I, I...'

Flash!

'Oh, was that it?' I ask Wesley.

83

He is shaking his head and smiling. He is shaking his head but he says, 'That's it.'

He starts laughing. Patrick looks upset but then I slap him on the back and he starts laughing and I start laughing.

'Shall we do it again?' I ask.

'Hurry up in there!' someone shouts.

'There's someone waiting,' says Patrick.

'I don't care, let them wait!' I say.

I think I must have said it too loud as the woman pulls back the curtain and puts her face to my face and says, 'Get out, slag!'

She has highlights and she is fat.

'Don't talk to her like that,' says Patrick.

The woman takes her head out and says something else but I don't hear it. We put the money in again but it's not so much fun the second time and when we get out the fat woman with highlights is staring at us. I walk past.

'Wait for the photos!' says Patrick and we have to stand outside and wait for them.

They take ages and the fat woman with highlights gets out and stands waiting for her photos as well. I stand in front of her. She's not nicking my photos.

The photos pop out and I go to take them.

'Wait! They're not dry!' says Patrick.

A blower comes on like a hair dryer and then it stops.

'You can take it now,' says Wesley.

There are one, two, three, four pictures. Two are of the back of my head and two are of the back of Patrick's head. I burst out laughing. So does Patrick. So does Wesley. Then another strip pops out and we wait for the photo dryer. The fat woman with highlights tuts but I'm not rushing for her.

'Hurry up!' she shouts but I wait for it to dry properly.

Sharon says it's important to take your time and do things properly. Sharon says Rome wasn't built in a day. I don't think anything is built in a day except a snowman or a sandcastle but not a building.

84

There are no backs of my head or Patrick's head in these four pictures but they are not very nice photos. Patrick is smiling but I am not smiling and Wesley is not smiling. We look fed up but we should look happy because we are in love and love makes you happy except when you love each other too much.

Mum is on the sofa with the bottle people again when I get in but this time I hear noises from the kitchen. Steve is playing rock music and I hear voices of other men.

'Look who it is!' Steve says when he sees me. 'It's the lovely Jane.'

I don't like how he is saying it. He is talking and smiling at the same time and it makes his mouth look scary. The other men turn to look at me.

'Oi, oi!' says one. He has a red face and his belly is hanging over his jeans.

'Blimey, who's this then?' says another one. 'This Angie's daughter, is it?'

My head goes hot.

White trainers. Blue car. White van. Black dog. Red collar.

Everything is spinning.

'You been drinking? You want some more?'

Everything is spinning.

I hold the wall.

The photos fall out of my pocket onto the floor. I see Patrick's smiling face and Wesley and me looking sad.

Steve looks at the photos.

He stops smiling.

He bends down and picks them up.

I stop breathing.

The Misfits

18

Marilyn Monroe had lots of pictures taken of her. Everyone loves to look at her pictures. She was a model before she was an actress so she was used to cameras flashing at her. I bet she never got the back of her head in a photo by mistake. When she was a model, she had some pictures taken without any clothes on. There is a famous one, where she is lying on a red silk sheet. She is naked but you can't see anything rude. Not like a porno magazine that you can buy from the top shelf of *Smiths* like some men have at the day centre and hide under the desk when Sharon or other staff come in.

I have got a book of her in my flat with lots of pictures in. That is my favourite kind of book. I don't like books with lots of words because they are hard. I can read some words, like names or months or recipes. My Marilyn Monroe book is my favourite book. She is laughing in most of the photos in the book. In some, she is putting her makeup on in the mirror. In one, she is lying on the bed, talking on the phone. There are lots of photos of her on a beach. In one, she is wearing a big woolly cardigan pulled over a bikini and she is walking in the sea with bare feet. She looks cold. In one, she is running and jumping in the sea wearing a peach bikini and she laughing and the waves are splashing. In one, she is wearing the same bikini and she is lying on the sand. The beach photos are my favourite photos because I love the beach.

I smile at the girl sitting opposite me on the train. She has bleached blonde hair like me and she smiles back. She has a purple rucksack on the seat next to her and she is reading a paper and drinking a cup of coffee from a paper cup. I haven't got a rucksack with me but I have got my handbag and I have got a bit of money but not much. It doesn't matter because all my things are back in my flat, near the beach in Cranley Crescent in Southend, where I can walk along the pier and throw pebbles in the sea and play on slot machines and eat sticks of rock and visit Penny and Gillian and my best friend, Joan. I am not staying in Dagenham with Mum and Steve any more.

When I get home to my flat, I am going to make myself a cup of tea, just the way I like it, in my Marilyn Monroe mug and I am going to stir it with my teaspoon with the tiny picture of her head on the end. I am going to have a bath in my blue bath where no-one else's dirty bum has been and where I can light all the candles I want. I am going to make myself a pizza with pineapple or I might just buy one if I am too tired because I am starting to feel very tired now. I am going to get into my bed with my lilac duvet covers and go to sleep. And in the morning, I am going to put on the clothes I like, not the stupid itchy roll-necks that Mum wants me to wear.

I am not going back to Dagenham. I am not going to live at Mum and Steve's house again. No-one can make me because I am an adult and I can make my own choices and it is stupid anyway because I have my own flat in Cranley Crescent and I am going back there. If Rose says I have to go back, I will say no. I will tell her that it's all stupid because Natasha didn't do anything wrong and Mum just didn't like her because she thought she was a punk and Rose will have to let me stay in my flat and she'll have to let Natasha come and help me twice a week and maybe we can do social support and see the Jennifer Lopez film.

I get off the train and I take a big breath.
I can smell the sea.
I can hear seagulls.
I can see the shops.
I am home.
I feel so happy.
I walk down the road to Cranley Crescent. When Rose first got me the flat, it took me time to get to know where it

was. The first time I went out on my own, I forgot the way back. I went out to the shops to look around and I couldn't remember what roads to walk back down. I got scared and had to ask someone in the street if they knew where Cranley Crescent was. I asked an old man with a shopping trolley and he walked with me to the top of my road. I said thank you, did he want to come in for a cup of tea but he said I should be careful about asking people in who I didn't know. He asked me who looked after me and I told him I look after myself. Then he walked away.

I am at the corner of Cranley Crescent and I start to cry. This is where I live. I look at all the doors of the flats in a row. It is a very small road. It is called a project. You can only live in the project if Rose says so because she is in charge. I look at Frank's blue door and I hear the television through the window. He has it up loud because he can't hear very well. I look at the pot plant outside Joan and Paul's flat. The flowers are pink and white but they are dying. I look at Penny and Gillian's door and it opens. Penny is standing there looking surprised.

'Gillian! Gillian! She's back! She's back!'

'Oh.' Gillian appears beside her.

'Ha. Haaaaaaaaaaaaaaaaa! She's back! Marilyn's back.'

Penny rushes out of the flat and runs towards me. I am so happy to see her. She follows me to my door and I open my bag to get the key and then I remember. Rose took it back off me when she came to visit me in hospital. Just temporary, she said, until we sort this out. I stamp my foot. I start crying more.

'Oh,' says Gillian. 'What are you going to do?'

Penny rushes back into their flat and comes back.

'Shouldn't really. Shouldn't really. Rose said to keep it safe. Safe! Ha!!!'

She is holding a key.

'Don't know when she came. No! No, no. Boxes everywhere. Everywhere!! I said it's Marilyn's. Didn't she?'

'Oh.' Gillian looks at the key then at me.

It is the spare key to my flat. I forgot they had that key. When we first moved in, Rose made us choose someone else in the crescent to look after a spare key, in case we got locked out.

I take it.

I open the door.

I am home.

19

Everything is different than before. My Marilyn Monroe calendar is not on the wall in the hall where it should be. I cannot see it anywhere and it makes tears come into my eyes. Who has taken it? I look at Gillian in the doorway. She doesn't say anything but her eyes are big. Penny is running around outside talking to herself. She is making a lot of noise but I am not listening to what she is saying. I am looking at my flat. I walk inside and Gillian walks behind me. Everything is different. The phone with the emergency star button has yellow post-it notes stuck on it. They are not my notes. I pick one up. It is a phone number. I don't know whose number it is but it makes my head hurt very bad. I feel like I can't breathe.

'Oh,' says Gillian.

She takes something out of her pocket and gives it to me.

'Do you want this?'

I look at it. It is a brown tube. It is what she has to breathe when she gets asthma.

I shake my head.

The mirror above the phone has stickers on it. The stickers are of footballers. They are not my stickers.

I look at Gillian. She looks at me. She doesn't say anything.

I look at the end of the hall. There is a sports bag on the floor, like one you would take to the gym or swimming. I have a pink sports bag that I take to the day centre. I haven't been to the day centre for a long time. This bag is white with black stripes. It is not my bag. It makes my heart beat very fast. You have to be very careful if you see a bag and you don't know whose it is. It could be a bomb. It could have a knife inside. It could be anything.

I run back to the phone and press the star.

'Oh, oh,' says Gillian.

'Help! Help! Someone has broken into my flat!' I shout into the phone but it is ringing. You have to wait for the person to answer before you speak. You have to wait. You have to wait.

Penny is in the hall.

'Rose said, didn't she? I told her. I told her. Boxes of clothes, so many for dancing. What's her name? She mustn't, must she? No. NO.'

Someone answers the phone. It is a man. I don't know his voice. I don't know him. The door at the end of the hall opens and I slam the phone down. I should not have done this because someone has broken into my flat and they might have a bomb or a knife and the man who answers emergencies has gone. The man who isn't Natasha or Rose has gone. The door at the end of the hall opens. I scream. Gillian grabs onto me and she screams too. Penny runs up behind us and shouts very loud, so many words, I don't know what she is saying.

There is a girl standing there. Her face is very white like she has seen a ghost but I am not a ghost. I am a real person and I live here in this flat. I live here. This is my flat, not her flat. She is very white like she is a ghost. Maybe she is a ghost. Maybe she is the ghost of someone who lived there a long time ago and died in the bed. Maybe she got stabbed in the bed and now she has a knife in her bag and she is going to stab me so that she can come back and live here again. Maybe she has been living here since I went to stay at Mum and Steve's. Maybe she doesn't want me to come back. She won't let me.

When people die you can still see them sometimes and they can still talk to you if they want to but you can't make them talk to you. I still see Janey and I talk to her but she doesn't talk to me much. Sometimes she laughs or sometimes she cries to let me know if she is happy or sad but that is all. Once I saw Aunt Maggie after she died and I was living at Mummy Barbara's and I couldn't go to sleep because I had the wrong pillows and I can only sleep with a fluffy pillow not a flat pillow and Maggie knew that. She came into my room and she told me it was okay, she would still look after me forever and ever, even though she was dead. She told me I had to ask my new mummy to get the right pillow, so that's what I did.

I would like to meet Marilyn Monroe's ghost but I haven't seen her yet. You can't make the spirits come. That's what Joan says. She believes in ghosts, too. She talks to her mum and dad and dead baby. Joan says we shouldn't tell people that we believe in ghosts because they will think we are crazy and want to lock us up. We are not crazy because everyone knows that there are ghosts really but they don't want to believe it because it makes them scared. They don't have to be scared because not all ghosts are evil. Some ghosts are good and some are bad. Like people.

I wonder if the girl with the white face is good or bad.

'Who are you?' she asks me.

I think maybe she might not be a ghost because her face is turning red.

'My name is Marilyn,' I tell her. 'Who are you?'

'I'm, I'm Karen.' I think she is scared. She talks like she is scared. I don't want to make her scared.

'Oh,' says Gillian and she looks at me and looks at me again. 'She's Karen.'

'KAREN. HA, ha, ha haaaaaaaa. That's it! K-A-R-E-N. I told her, didn't I, didn't I say?'

Karen looks at Penny. I think she is scared of Penny not me.

'Wh-what d-do you w-want?' she asks me.

'I don't want anything,' I say.

We look at each other's eyes. Her eyes are lots of different colours. They are grey and brown and green and blue. They keep changing colour like her face is changing from white to red. I look at the rest of her head and her body. Her hair is long and brown in a ponytail. Her body is a bit fat but not very fat. She is wearing a tee-shirt but she must be very cold. I don't understand why she is asking me what I want.

'Why are you here?' I ask her.

'Rose said.'

She still looks scared.

'Rose said what?' I ask.

'Rose said I can live here to see.'

I kick her bag and she jumps. I don't want to make her scared but I can't stop. I kick it and kick it and kick it.

'Rose can't say that! Rose can't say that! This is my flat! You can't live here! You can't live here!'

I kick it and kick it and kick it. It knocks over onto the side and lots of things fall out onto the floor. Karen's brush and pen and socks and tampons are on my floor in my flat. She can't live here.

'You can't!' I shout at her.

I hit the wall. She moves back. Her eyes are changing colour again. She is crying. My cheeks are wet. I am crying too.

'Oh, I, I…' Karen bends down to pick up her brush and pen and socks and tampons from my floor.

Penny is laughing.

Gillian has put her hand in my hand and she is squeezing my hand.

'It's only a test,' says Karen from the floor. 'To see.'

Penny starts jumping. 'To see! To see! Ha haaaa!'

I don't understand.

'What's a test?'

Karen stands up again. She stops crying and she sticks her chin out.

'Rose said I could have a week's trial. She said the person that lived here was staying somewhere else for a little while so I could stay here for a week's trial to see if I could live on my own. She said I might be able to get a flat of my own like this one, if I do well.'

Karen looks past me and Gillian and Penny and waves to

someone outside walking past the front door. I turn round
and look out the front door.
   It is Joan.
   She doesn't see me.

20

I run out the door to see Joan but I am too late because she has gone into her own flat with Paul and closed the front door. I stand outside her door and I hold up my hand to knock on the door but I don't know what to do. I am crying so much that I can't see anything and my neck feels wet. I hate Karen. She wants my flat. She has taken it. She has taken my Marilyn Monroe calendar and I am never going to get it back. She wants my best friend. She is waving at my best friend, who doesn't even see me. She wants to take everything away from me. I hate her. I wish she was a ghost because then she'd be dead. I hate her. I hate her. I hate everyone. Sharon says hate is a strong word and when we say it we don't really mean it but I do mean it.

I hate Rose for making me live at Mum and Steve's and for letting Karen live there without even asking me and for letting her take my Marilyn Monroe calendar down and stick football stickers on the mirror and for making Natasha go. Rose is not my friend. I hate Joan for waving at Karen and not me. I hate Steve for looking at me like in that horrible way and for talking to me in that horrible way and for hitting Mum. I hate Mum for letting Steve live with her and letting him hit her and letting him look at me in that horrible way and for drinking all the time and for giving me away just because I didn't work properly. I hate Aunt Maggie for dying, even though I know she couldn't help it but then I had to live with Mummy Barbara and Mummy Lynn and I didn't like it because I wanted to be with her. I hate Barbara for not having the right pillows for my bed and not keeping me.

I hate Gail for not letting me stay in her spare room even though she doesn't want her mum to stay there. She is not my friend. I hate Keith for chucking me and not even telling me. I hate his dad for looking at my bra. I hate Penny for laughing all the time when there is nothing to laugh about. I hate the boys with white trainers who left me for dead on Christmas Eve. I hate everyone in the whole world and all the people that are in another world or dead or ghosts. Except Janey or Natasha or Marilyn Monroe.

I want to hit someone really hard. I want to go back and hit Karen and punch her face and make it red and purple and yellow but if I hit Karen they will call it anti-social behaviour and I might get in lots of trouble and I will never be allowed to live in my flat again and they might put me in the home, like John and Susan or they might lock me in prison, where I will never, ever, ever be allowed out and I will never see Wesley again and he doesn't even know where I am.

I turn away from Joan's house and I run and run and run. I hear Joan call me from behind but I keep running and running and running. I run out of Cranley Crescent and down all the other roads until I get to the High Road. I run past *Mothercare* and *Boots* and *Sainsbury's* and all the other shops and I keep running. I run past the station and I hear a train go by and my chest hurts. I run to the sea front and I stop and breathe. I can smell the sea and I breathe it all the way into my body so it makes me feel a bit better. But I still hate Karen and Rose and Steve.

I walk onto the beach and I feel my shoes crunching on the wet pebbles. The wind is blowing very hard and it is cold and there are not many people here. There is an old woman in a big coat walking a dog. There are some children running and laughing. And there is me. I have to find Natasha. She is my friend. She is my only friend. She will make everything alright. I know where she lives even though I am not supposed to because you are not supposed to go to your support worker's house.

Natasha says that some rules are silly because when I got soaked through in the rain because I forgot my umbrella and she bumped into me in the street and we were near her house, she said it would be nonsense to say I couldn't come in and get dry just because it was a rule. Her flat is painted bright green and blue and purple and every room is a different colour and she lives there with Seb. She gave me a towel and let me change into some of her clothes and she walked me back to my flat under Seb's big stripey umbrella. She never said we had to keep it a secret but I didn't tell anyone.

I go to her house and I press the buzzer for the top flat and I wait for her to answer. Somebody else lives in the flat underneath but I don't know them. She doesn't answer and neither does Seb but the door opens anyway. A man with a motorbike hat comes out and I go in. He looks at me but he doesn't ask me who I am. I walk up the stairs and I knock on the door to Natasha and Seb's flat. I knock very loud but no-one answers. I wait for what might be a short time or a long time and then I go back down the stairs and out the front door.

I walk back to the seafront and up Pier Hill to where all the amusement arcades are because I know that Seb works there, counting out coins behind a glass window. They all have funny names but I can't read them that well. Seb told me the names before. He works in Mr B's and sometimes Electric Avenue and Monte Carlo when he needs more shifts to get more money to go out with his boyfriend. There is lots of loud music playing and it comes right out onto the street as you walk by. You can hear coins falling out of machines and coins falling in.

I stop outside a teddy bear machine because I want to get one. It says one pound. I know the signs for money because Sharon taught them to me in shopping class. I open my handbag and take out my purse. I know what one pound is because that's easy. I put the pound in the slot and then the lights flash. There is a crane that you have to get the teddy with. There are lots of teddies of all different colours and I want a pink one. I move the crane to one side then the other side then back then forwards to get it in the right place. The crane goes down over the pink teddy and it closes on the teddy's arm but it slips out and falls back to the pile of teddies.

I kick the machine and someone shouts so I run off and go inside the next arcade.

There is a man with a skinhead and a horrible face putting money in a machine. I don't like coming into the arcades by myself. In the summer, there are lots of children and it is okay but when it is cold there are just horrible looking men and I don't know where Seb is. I go up to the glass window to see if he is there but it is someone else. A girl with black hair. She looks a bit like Natasha but she isn't Natasha. I go to the next and the next and the next arcade and the next arcade until I have been in all the arcades and I don't know how many there are.

'Whoa! Marilyn!' says Seb as he grabs my arms and he looks so happy to see me that I cry some more.

21

Seb's hair is all shaved off so I nearly didn't know it was him. Before, he had long hair in a pony tail like a girl's hair. His boyfriend, Johnny never had any hair but I think he only shaved his because he was going bald and he didn't want anyone to know, so he was pretending to be a skinhead so that people didn't think he was an old man.

Seb says that lots of gay men have skinheads but they are different from other kinds of skinheads, who like to wear Union Jacks and don't like gay men nicking their trademark. Seb says they don't like gay men full stop and they don't like black people either. I don't think Seb should have a skinhead. It is very confusing because how are you supposed to work out which skinheads are gay and which skinheads are the other sort?

Seb's job is counting out ten pence pieces for people who are addicted to slot machines. That's what he says. He says everyone is addicted to something but some things are worse than others. I don't know what I am addicted to. They say you can be addicted to love, don't they? I think Marilyn Monroe was addicted to love. I don't know about me. Sometimes I think I am addicted to love like when I am with Wesley and I want to be with him every minute of the day but other times I don't think I am like now because I am here and not with him.

'What are you doing here?' asks Seb.

Seb looks like he is running away from someone. His cheeks are all red and he is rushing. Maybe the skinheads were waiting for him outside Kim's Tattoo and Body Piercing Shop like that time before. Maybe he has had an argument with Johnny again like when Johnny threw the fruit bowl out the window on Seb's head and you could see all the different colours of the oranges and apples and peaches and bananas flying through the air and you could smell all the different smells of their juice as they hit the ground and squashed. Maybe it is me that is doing the running not Seb.

'I, I…' I can't remember why I am running.

I am very tired.

'Natasha told me they'd taken you back to your mum's?'

'I want to see Natasha.'

'I don't know if that's such a good idea,' says Seb.

'It is a good idea,' I say. 'It is a very good idea.'

People think that I can't have good ideas but that's a lie because I have lots of good ideas, like sorting out my washing with different colour clothes pegs. Red is for underwear. Blue is for bed linen. Green is for tea towels. White is for whites. Yellow is for all the other clothes. Natasha says I have lots of good ideas. She knows I have good ideas. She would know that it is a good idea to see her.

'It's just… well, I don't know if it's allowed. She told me about the complaint that your mum made and everything…'

'I am an adult and I can make my own choices. I don't have to do what my mum says.'

I think I say it very loud because a group of teenagers, who are addicted to slot machines, start looking over.

'Okay, okay. Let's go get a cup of tea,' says Seb.

'I don't want tea! I want Natasha!'

'Okay, okay, but Natasha's been very upset about it all,' he says, shaking his head. I think this means I can't see Natasha because if you shake your head it means no. Even if you don't say no, it still doesn't mean yes.

Seb starts walking down the road in front of me but he is sort of pulling me along by the hand and I don't like it because I don't know where he is taking me. I don't like being pulled along.

I shout, 'I want Natasha!'

Seb stops walking.

I see the old woman walking her dog, the one from the beach. He is big and hairy. She is walking towards us.

'Is everything okay, dear?' she asks when she gets to us.

'No, everything is not okay!'

She looks at me. She looks at Seb. The big hairy dog is barking.

'Oh. What's going on? Do you know this man?'

'Yes!'

'Look, with all due respect,' says Seb to the woman with the growling dog. 'It's probably better if you just leave us to get on with it. She's...'

I saw a blue car and a white van go past. I saw a black dog being walked. He wasn't big and hairy. He was small and fluffy and he had a brown collar not a red collar. A woman in a long coat was walking him and she looked at me but she didn't stop.

Seb and the woman with the dog are arguing.

'Yes, I can see that!' says the woman with the dog but I don't know what she can see.

'Look, she's upset. I'm taking her to see her support worker, that's all,' says Seb.

He's taking me to see Natasha!

I squeeze his hand.

'It's okay,' I tell the woman with the dog.

'Are you sure?'

I nod my head because I don't want my voice to come out too loud again but I think she thinks I am lying because she doesn't walk away so I start walking away instead and pull Seb along behind me.

'Blimey, girl!' he says, shaking his head. 'You'll be the death of me. Come on.'

I tell him that I've been to the house but Natasha isn't there.

'No, I know where she is,' he says.

'Where?'

'Tea,' he says.

I wish he would stop talking about tea because it is confusing me but I don't want to shout again, so I keep walking. He is taking me down the pier to the teashop that sells scones.

'Go easy on her,' he says. 'She's taken it all very badly.'

I don't understand what he is talking about. Natasha will make everything alright again.

We walk inside the tea shop and Seb nods his head and looks at me like he is pointing to someone with his head. There is a woman wearing black with her back to us sitting at a table on her own, drinking a cup of tea. It must be Natasha but I wouldn't have known that straight away because something looks different but I don't know what. Not like with Seb because that was easy to work out what was different because he shaved his hair off.

'Tash,' says Seb.

She turns round and her face looks sad. It is all scrunched up with lines like Mum gets when she is worried about Steve. I think my face is scrunched up too. When she sees me, she starts to smile and all the lines go smooth. Then they come back and her face gets sad again.

'W-what, what…'

I don't think she knows what to say.

I can see an empty plate with crumbs on it next to her cup of tea. I think she has been eating a lot of scones. Her face looks fat. Her hair is tied up but it is very messy and very greasy. If I let my hair go like that, Rose would say that I need to improve my personal hygiene skills. It is very important to do personal hygiene properly and be clean and tidy.

'I came to see you,' I say.

She looks at me like she is looking at a ghost, like I looked at Karen, like I shouldn't be here.

'Does anyone know that you're here?' she asks.

'You know I'm here.'

Seb is standing behind me. He taps me on the shoulder and says, 'I'm going to leave you guys to talk for a bit. I'll just be outside.'

As Young As You Feel

22

Marilyn Monroe never had a baby but she wanted one so much. She lost some of her babies before they were born. It is called a miscarriage and no-one knows why it happens. Natasha says it happens to lots of women early on, before anyone even knows they are pregnant. She says that is why the doctors say to wait three months before you tell anyone because you might lose it. It is different than what happened to Janey because she was alive when she was coming out, until she got strangled. It is different than what happened to Joan because the doctors killed her baby. It is called an abortion.

Natasha says that Marilyn Monroe had at least twelve abortions but I don't believe her. This is what happened to Joan at the special clinic when they did something to kill the baby and Joan was very sad. I don't believe that Marilyn Monroe killed her babies because she loved babies and everyone knows she wanted to have one of her own. If I was pregnant with a baby, I would love it and never let anyone kill it before it was born. I would love it and never give it away. I would never give it to someone else to take care of.

Natasha says it is complicated and you shouldn't judge people unless you have walked a mile in their shoes. I wouldn't like to walk a mile in Natasha's shoes because they are pointed black boots and they look uncomfortable, like they would give you blisters on your heels. She says that sometimes people get pregnant when they are too young and they can't cope. Or even if you're not that young, you might feel like a child yourself and not ready to be a mother. Do I understand what a big responsibility it is? She says that maybe Marilyn Monroe felt that she wasn't able to care for a child, even though she wanted one. She says maybe she needed to nurture her inner child but never got the chance. She says maybe she had to give birth to herself, before she could give birth to a baby.

She is making me feel funny. I told her that I hate Karen and Joan and Rose and Mum and Steve and everyone except her and she started saying all these things.

I look out the window and see Seb sitting at the end of the pier and throwing pebbles into the sea. It is dark outside. I don't know what the time is. I think maybe I want to go out and sit next to Seb and throw pebbles into the sea but Natasha is still talking. I told her about Karen being in my flat and that I was cross with Rose because it was my flat, not Karen's but I don't know if she was really listening. She kept stirring her tea with her teaspoon and licking her fingers and pressing them onto the crumbs on the plate and licking them off.

'God, I'm sorry, Marilyn. I shouldn't be telling you all this. It's not appropriate, I…' says Natasha but I don't know what she is telling me. 'I've been off sick since… A lot of stuff came up for me that I'd buried and I've had to deal with it. I still am dealing with it. Not very well, though. God, how are you coping?'

'Oh,' I say. She does look sick. Her face is grey. She looks sick and fat. 'What's wrong with you? Have you got the flu?'

'No, I haven't got the flu,' she says.

She stops stirring and licking and her eyes look at my eyes. Her eyes look at my face. They look at every little bit of my face like she has never seen my face before, or it is something very interesting, like when Sharon took us on a trip to a gallery and we stared at the pictures because we didn't know what we were suppose to be looking for. Natasha picks up my hands and holds them both. Her hands feel sticky. I think about Wesley and I wish he was holding my hands instead of Natasha.

'You know when you feel really bad, like if you are angry or upset or sad?' she says.

I nod my head because I do know. I feel angry and upset and sad that Karen is in my flat.

'Well, you know sometimes if you feel bad in your mind, it can make you feel bad in your body, like give you a headache or a stomach ache?'

I nod my head because I do know.

'Well, sometimes if you feel very very bad, it can make you ill. Not just a headache but really ill.'

I don't like her saying that because I don't want it to happen to me. I don't want to be really ill, so I think I'd better stop feeling bad.

'That's what happened to me,' she says.

'Oh,' I say.

I didn't think that support workers or people who are staff could get really ill. But Natasha isn't like other staff. I know that she feels bad sometimes, like when she cried in my kitchen.

'When your mum said all those things about me not looking after you properly, I didn't know what to think,' she says.

'I don't need looking after,' I say and I take my hands away and wipe them on my jeans. 'I am an adult and I can look after myself.'

'Yes, I know. That's what I thought, what I do think. You are an adult. But you do need help, right? You do need help to be safe and to look after yourself.'

'So!' I say.

'I mean you couldn't live on your own without any help, could you? You do need help so, so, you need protection, you need…'

'I could!' I shout. 'I could do it!'

The woman in the pink polka dot apron behind the counter looks over and whispers something to the woman in the stripy apron next to her.

'What are you looking at?' I say and the woman wipes her hands on her apron and turns away.

'Marilyn, Marilyn, I didn't mean to upset you, I, I'm…'

Natasha's eyes look down. I wish she would look at my

111

eyes.

'Everyone needs help,' I say and I take her hands again, even though they are sticky, because I think maybe she needs me to help her but I don't know what I can do to help her.

Joan said I am her best friend because she can always turn to me for help, like when she is upset and wants a shoulder to cry on. Like after they killed her baby or she had an argument with Paul about money or something. That was before Karen moved into my flat and Joan started waving at Karen and not at me. I think maybe Natasha might want to cry on my shoulder too because she looks so sad.

'Yes, yes. They do,' she says and she looks at my eyes again and laughs.

'What's funny?' I ask.

'Oh, I don't know. Nothing. It's not funny at all.'

She laughs again and it makes me laugh.

'What?' I ask.

'I just think… well, I'm the support worker and you're the client, right?'

I nod my head and I look outside at Seb throwing pebbles. He turns around and waves.

'Well, why is that? Who says I can support anyone? What gives me the right? What…'

I don't really like the way Natasha is talking. She is making me feel funny, like when she cried in my kitchen like she isn't a proper support worker but I don't want to say that to her because I think it might make her cry. I sort of do like it, as well. Sometimes you can like something that makes you feel funny and scared, like if you go on a roller coaster but not if you are sick afterwards. I feel a bit sick now, like there is lots of water coming into my mouth. I swallow hard to make it stop.

'… then I got confused. I thought maybe your mum was right. Maybe it was my fault you got attacked.'

She stops talking and her eyes look from one of my eyes to the other. From side to side. Like she is looking for

112

something inside my eyes. I don't know what she is looking for. I don't understand what she is talking about. But I like it that she doesn't think she is more important than me, like Rose does, who tells other girls that they can live in my flat.

'Maybe, I haven't been very good at my job. Maybe, I'm just not cut out for this type of work.'

'I think you are good,' I say. 'You are good fun and it's okay to be sad sometimes, isn't it? That's what you told me.'

She smiles at me.

'You've got quite fat, though,' I say.

'I know,' she says and smiles but it is a sad smile and a tear comes out of her eye and rolls down her cheek.

'Anything else, love?' asks the woman in the apron with a notepad. She is looking at her watch.

'Oh, erm, you haven't even had a drink!' says Natasha. 'Do you want a cup of tea or something?'

I am very thirsty so I nod my head.

'Two teas, please,' says Natasha to the woman in the apron.

'TWO TEAS!' shouts the woman in the apron to another woman behind the counter, then she starts walking off. She doesn't look very happy with us.

'What about food? Have you had anything to eat, Marilyn? How long have you been here? God, I haven't even checked that you're alright. I haven't...'

I don't know when I last had any food or drink. I can't remember when this morning was, the day seems to have been going on forever and ever and ever.

'I could eat some chips,' I say.

'Oh, God, me too,' says Natasha. 'I know I shouldn't but... Excuse me?'

The woman in the apron turns round.

'Yes,' she says sighing.

'Can we have two portions of chips as well, please?'

'TWO CHIPS!'

'I feel very confused, Marilyn. Do you understand what I am talking about?'

113

'No,' I say.

Natasha laughs.

'I don't suppose you do, when I don't even understand myself.'

The woman brings two cups of tea on saucers and two plates of chips that smell so good they make the water start coming in my mouth again. Natasha says thank you but I don't, because I think the woman in the apron is rude because you shouldn't stare at people or whisper behind their back.

'You've coped so well with so many things, Marilyn,' says Natasha and it makes me laugh. It makes me very happy. 'You are very wise, much wiser than me.'

I shake salt and vinegar on my chips and squirt ketchup on top and eat the biggest chip first. I am not feeling angry anymore. Seb is trying to say something to us through the window but I can't understand what he is trying to say. He is running towards the door and he pushes it open.

'Hey, thanks for asking!' he says, as he nicks two of my chips at once.

'Sorry,' says Natasha. 'Have some of mine. I shouldn't be eating them any way.'

'So how are my two favourite girls feeling, now? You both look a hell of a lot better than before you got talking so that's got to be a good thing, right?'

'I think I'm pregnant,' I say.

23

'Shit! That's heavy,' says Seb and he takes the chip back out of his mouth and holds it in the air.

I put my hands on my belly.

'I'm not heavy. I'm not even big, yet. When I get really big, I won't be able to wear my jeans.'

He laughs and then stops. Natasha is giving him a look, like he has done something wrong.

'Have you done a pregnancy test?' asks Natasha and she pushes her plate away, even though she hasn't finished all her chips.

Maybe Natasha has started on a diet, from now. That is good because people normally say they will start the diet tomorrow and they keep on eating bad things and they never start the diet tomorrow, like when Mum says she will stop drinking tomorrow but she doesn't, because the next day she says she will stop drinking tomorrow, and the next day she says it again. Sharon says it is important to eat a balanced diet. That doesn't mean you have to go on a diet but it's important to be healthy and not eat takeways every day but once in a while is okay. A balanced diet has lot of fruit and vegetables because they are very good for you and make you go to the toilet but you can have other things too. Sharon says a little of what you fancy won't kill you.

Joan had to go on a diet because she got very fat because she kept eating lots of bad things all the time and the doctor said she might get a heart attack if she kept going the way she was going, so a lot of what you fancy will kill you, even if a little of what you fancy won't. Joan went on a *Weight Watchers* Diet but it was very difficult because you had to count lots of points to work it out. Sharon said it might be better to make up her own special diet together, so Sharon helped her do some recipe cards with points on top. If you have a bowl of soup, it might be one point or two points.

I have never been on a diet because I think I have a nice body. I don't want to be too thin because I think women are supposed to be curvy, like Marilyn Monroe. They call her an hourglass figure, which means an egg timer because her body looks like the shape of an egg timer. It is round at the top and the bottom and thin in the middle. Wesley says I have the most beautiful body he has ever seen. I miss Wesley. I don't know when I am going to see him again.

'Marilyn? Have you done a pregnancy test?' Natasha is talking like a support worker again.

I shake my head and keep eating my chips, until I see they are all gone.

'Can I have some more chips?' I ask.

'Can you remember when you last had your injection?'

'They say you have to eat for two, don't they? Does that mean I can have two dinners instead of one?'

'Marilyn,' says Natasha.

The woman in the polka dot apron is looking at her watch.

'I think we should go,' says Seb.

'Yeah, okay,' says Natasha and she goes to pay at the counter.

Seb follows her. I don't know where we are going to go. Natasha is talking to Seb and she looks cross at him and then he looks cross at her. I don't know who has done something wrong.

'Does your mum know you are here in Southend?' asks Natasha, as we walk outside.

It is very cold. I wish I was wearing a roll-neck jumper. I can go back to my flat in Cranley Crescent and get a jumper but not a roll-neck because I don't have any of those, except the ones at Mum's house. I don't want to go back to Mum and Steve's.

'Marilyn?'

'I am an adult and I can make my own choices,' I say.

'Yes, Marilyn. You are an adult but even adults have to let people know where they are and what they are doing.'

I don't want to go back to Mum and Steve's.

'Does your mum know where you are?' I ask her and then I look at Seb and ask him too, 'Or your mum?'

'Yes, my mum knows I am here in Southend,' says Natasha. 'She might not like it but she knows.'

'And yours?' I ask Seb.

'Whoa, look girls, keep me out of this, please.'

'Whatever I think or feel about your mum, she's still your mum,' says Natasha but it is getting confusing. 'She'll be worried, won't she?'

'No, she'll be with the bottle people on the sofa.'

Natasha looks at Seb and I am scared that they are going to make me go back to Mum and Steve's.

'I'm NOT GOING!!!!!!' I scream.

'Okay, okay, okay,' says Natasha. 'Okay, Marilyn. Let's calm down. No-one's going to make you do anything, okay?'

I nod but I don't move, even though Natasha has put her arm through my arm and is trying to make me walk.

'It's getting very late. Now, we need to work out what we're going to do here, okay?'

'Don't look at me,' says Seb.

Natasha gives him another cross look.

'I think we'll have to go back to the flat, won't we? Yes, yes,' she says.

'Okay, we're going back to my flat. We're going to get Karen out,' I say.

'No,' says Natasha. 'I mean, well, maybe you will be going back but let's just go back to our flat for now and decide how to sort this out just for now, okay?'

'So I can live in your flat?'

'Well, not live, no. You know that wouldn't be allowed. Just go back there for a cup of tea and...'

I don't want tea. I want more chips.

I know Natasha is still talking but I can't listen. My head hurts and I want to go to sleep. Joan says I'm a good listener but I don't want to listen. I don't feel good at anything.

117

24

There are lots of different kinds of injections. I know because the doctor told me at the medical centre in Southend. Sometimes Rose or Sharon or Natasha went to the doctor with me but sometimes I went on my own because I knew where to go and the doctor was nice. Her name was Doctor Singer, but she didn't sing, but she did have a nice voice and she always called me Marilyn. If I went on my own, Sharon or Natasha helped me with my calendar, so I went on the right day and didn't miss it and they checked up on me, like if I had to go on Tuesday then Natasha would ask me on Wednesday if I had gone and I had to show her my card. I know that Wednesday comes after Tuesday because it says so on the calendar. It comes after Tuesday every week.

Some injections are for people who are going on holiday to a different country, in an aeroplane. When I was waiting to see the doctor, there was a woman in a long dress, like Rose used to wear and she was reading a magazine and she kept looking at me, like she wanted to talk to me. I said hello because it's important to be polite to people if they look at you and she told me she was going on holiday to something called Goa and that's why she was at the doctor's because she had to have lots of injections to stop her getting ill in Goa and she was a bit scared of injections but she didn't care because she was so excited about her holiday.

A nurse came and called out her name. It was Marjorie. Marjorie went with the nurse to have her injections, to stop her getting ill in Goa and then I didn't have anyone to talk to and I had to wait a long time for the doctor to come and call my name so I picked up the magazine that Marjorie was reading and I looked at the pictures. I like looking at pictures because it is easier than looking at words. There was a picture of clothes that you can take on holiday like a bikini. That is like wearing underwear outdoors but you are allowed to wear it on the beach or a swimming pool. I don't like swimming though because I'm not very good at it and I don't want to wear arm bands because they are for babies.

I asked the doctor why Marjorie had to have injections to go to Goa and she said that it was because there are different illnesses in different countries and what they do is they put a little bit of the illness in your arm with the needle and if they give you a little bit of it, you won't get a lot of the illness. I think it is very complicated because doctors are very clever and important people, that's why Gail wants Jake to be a doctor and the Chinese man behind the counter, whose daughter is Mai, wants her to be a doctor too. I told Doctor Singer that I didn't want anyone to put a little bit of an illness in my arm. Doctor Singer laughed at me and said that I already had it done when I was little, but with different illnesses called mumps and measles and something else.

Some injections are medicine to calm you down like Joan had at the special clinic when they killed her baby. They give injections that calm you down to mad people, who have to be locked up in mental hospitals, like Marilyn Monroe's mum. I think that is very horrible and I don't want to ever be locked up in a hospital or a home, where you aren't allowed to go out and see your friends and you have to have injections, all day. Injections are horrible because they are needles that stick in you and they hurt.

Some injections are to stop babies growing. That is the injections that I have to have. I don't have to have them because I am an adult and I can make my own choices. But when I moved into Cranley Crescent, I had to have a long talk with Rose because she's in charge and Rose said I should have it, even though she said I don't have to do anything I don't want. She kept talking lots of words again and again and I said okay because I wanted to move into the flat and I wanted Rose to think I was good. Rose came with me the first time and she came in with me to see Doctor Singer. I remember because she was talking to Doctor Singer like they were

119

friends and she said she was going to see her the next day.

Sometimes, I am good at remembering things, like I can remember the colour of Mummy Barbara's eyes. They were all different colours - brown, grey, green and blue - and they changed colour if she was angry or if she was happy. She didn't get angry lots but she did get angry when I bit her on the leg and she locked me in my room and I didn't like it. Sometimes, I am good at remembering but sometimes, I am very bad at remembering and I can't remember things in the same day or what I am supposed to be doing, like if I go out to buy bread and I might forget and go and get my hair cut.

I do remember the first time I had to have the injection because I wet myself a little bit on the chair in Doctor Singer's room and then I cried. Rose was holding my hand and she told me to look at her and not at the needle going in but I couldn't do it right and I kept looking because I wanted to see what they were doing to me. I don't like people doing things to me that I can't see. I couldn't do it right because when the needle was coming to get me I pulled my arm away so Doctor Singer couldn't do it. I tried and I tried really, really hard not to pull my arm away.

Doctor Singer said we should leave it for today and try again when I had calmed down a bit, so that's what we did and Rose took me to the café and we had sausages and mash and then I went home, to take off my knickers and put new ones on because I had wet myself a little bit on the chair in Doctor Singer's room. I felt very bad because someone else like Marjorie might have to sit on the chair after I had wet myself a little bit on it but Marjorie wouldn't have to because she saw the nurse instead.

Rose took me back the next day and I looked at the chair. It was orange like the ones in the day centre. It didn't look wet then but I don't know if anyone had washed it. I sat on the chair and rolled up my sleeve and then Rose asked me what I wanted to have for lunch and I told her I wanted pizza and Doctor Singer said, 'All done', and I said, 'What?'.

120

Doctor Singer said she had done the injection already and see it wasn't so bad, was it? I couldn't believe it but it was true. So that's what we did the next time and that time I said I wanted chicken.

When Rose stopped coming and Sharon or Natasha did it instead, Rose told them they had to ask me to talk about what I wanted for lunch and we always had lunch together, after I had the needle done. I didn't like going on my own so much because then I had no-one to have lunch with.

25

'So you haven't had the injection at all since you moved back to your mum's?' says Natasha.

I thought Natasha was going to get cross with me when I told her that I lied to mum about going to the doctor for the injection and I lied to Rose about it when she phoned, but she isn't being cross. She is being like a support worker. We are in the bathroom at Natasha and Seb's flat. It is painted bright blue and has big white fishes all over the wall but the bath is white not like my blue bath in my flat.

'And you haven't had a period at all?'

'Not since MacDonald's.'

'And you're not sure when that was?'

'It was when Zig was horrible to me and Wesley was nice to me,' I say.

'Do you think it was more than a month ago?'

The fishes have silver painted on their backs. It is called fins. There are some silver starfish painted on the side of the bath. I like them.

'Can you help me do those on my bath?' I ask Natasha.

'Marilyn, I need you to focus on what I am asking you,' says Natasha. She's not cross but she is in charge. 'Do you think it was more than a month ago?'

'What day is it today?' I ask.

'It's the twentieth of March.'

Natasha is sitting on the floor in the bathroom on a rug and I am sitting on the toilet seat, with my clothes on.

'I don't know because Karen took my Marilyn Monroe calendar and Steve ripped up my other one.'

'Right, okay and you've definitely had full sex since your last period?'

'I think I know if I had sex or not,' I say because I might forget lots of things but I wouldn't forget having sex with Wesley but anyway it was making love not sex. 'I love

Wesley.'

'Okay, okay. Well, anyway it can take a while for periods to go back to normal after you stop the injection, so try not to worry. I think we should do the test now, okay?'

Try not to worry.

If I was pregnant with a baby, I would love it and never let anyone kill it before it was born. I would love it and never give it away. I would never give it to someone else to take care of.

I am worried.

'Are you ready?'

Natasha made Seb go to the chemist and buy the test on the way back, when she took me to the flat. She made me drink two cups of tea in a row because you have to do a wee to make the test work and I didn't want to do one. I shrug my shoulders because I think I am ready to do a wee but I don't know if I am ready to do the test. Natasha is holding the box with the test in it. She has lots of silver rings on her hands.

'Could you help me look after the baby?' I ask her.

Natasha puts the box down and holds my hands.

'Marilyn, let's do the test, okay?'

'But would you help me?'

'Marilyn, I…'

'Would you?'

Natasha is the support worker, so she is in charge, but she can't make me do the test until I am ready.

'I can't answer that, Marilyn.'

'Why?'

'Because there are too many unknowns.'

I hate it when she talks like that. One of her rings is a star like the starfish on her bath.

'What does that mean?'

'It means we don't even know if you're pregnant yet.'

'But if I am!' My head is hurting again.

'Please, Marilyn. Let's do the test. It's very late and you

123

must be tired. We need to do the test.'

She picks up the box again.

'What would you do if you were pregnant?' I ask her. 'Would you have the baby or would you let someone kill it or take it away?'

Natasha looks up at me and then she stands up and opens the box. I think she is cross now.

'We have to do the test now,' she says.

Rose told me that you are not allowed to ask staff personal questions like, do you have a boyfriend, or are you upset, or things like that, but I don't think that's fair because they ask you lots of personal questions worse than that.

'Would you?'

'Marilyn.' I know she is cross now because of the lines on her forehead and the way her shoulders have gone high up. 'I'm not going to answer that. This is not about me. It's about you. Now, please do the test.'

I don't like tests. Tests are when you have to do something and you might get it wrong or right, like spelling or maths. If you get it wrong, it means you are stupid. We did lots of tests at school and that's how they worked out if you were stupid or not. That's how they worked out I had a learning disability and I had to have special help. That's how they worked out I had to go to Mrs Taylor's Remedial Readers, with books with lots of pictures in and not many words and bright blue stickers on the front. Mrs Taylor said I was lucky that I was allowed to stay at Cannon School and not go to a special school but I don't know about that.

'I'm not doing a wee in front of you, Natasha.'

You're not even allowed to ask support workers if they would keep their baby but they are allowed to ask you to do a wee in front of them.

'Okay. Well, we need to make sure you understand the instructions then.'

Natasha takes the leaflet out of the box and reads it, then she takes out a stick thing that looks like a pen and she takes the lid off but I know it isn't a pen. It is a test to find out if I am going to have a baby or not.

'Okay, this is going to be easy, okay?'

'Hmmm.'

I don't know if it is going to be easy. Sometimes people say things are going to be easy and then they are hard, when Mrs Taylor said that level one books are going to be easy and that was a lie. Only the pictures were easy not the words. Words are not easy because they don't make sense. The letter 't' makes a 't' noise but if you put 'h' next then it does something else. That is why it is hard because it all keeps changing.

Natasha shows me the pictures on the leaflet and shows me the stick.

'You have to hold this bit, like that, underneath yourself on the toilet, so you wee on it, okay?'

'Hmmm.'

'You need to try and do it for a few seconds so you have to keep it still.'

'Mmm.'

'Are you sure you want to do this on your own?'

'Yes.'

'Okay. Well, I'll leave you to it and then you can call me when you're done. How does that sound?'

'Then what?'

'Then it will tell you there whether or not you are pregnant.'

'Oh.'

'So are you okay to do it now?'

'Yes.'

Natasha goes out of the door. Janey is watching me and she is putting me off. I always like to see Janey but today I wish she would go away. I try to get the stick in the right place. I think it is the right place but it might be the wrong place. I try to do the wee but it won't come and I think I might need another cup of tea but I don't want to go and get

Natasha because I want to do it right. It isn't easy to do it right. I start to wee but then it keeps stopping and I don't think I can do it right. If I can't do the test right they might not let me keep the baby, so I have to do it right. They might make me go to the special clinic like Joan but I won't let them.

Dangerous Years

26

Marilyn Monroe would have been a good mother. I don't care what people say because I know it is true. She would have loved her baby and not given it away. I think she would have had a little girl and she would have given her a pretty name like Annabelle or Isabelle and she would have dressed her up in a frilly dress, with a matching hat and booties and mittens, so it wouldn't get cold and pushed it round the park in a pram. She would have talked to Isabelle when she was just a tiny baby in her belly. She would have talked and sung to Isabelle through her tummy and she would have called her Issy because it is short for Isabelle and it is a secret name, like Janey. She would have sung lullabies to Issy to get her to sleep.

She would have given her a bath every day with bubbles in the water and rubber ducks and she would kiss Issy on the forehead before she put her in the bath and if she didn't know how hot the bath had to be she would get someone to help her, like a support worker or someone from the day centre. Sharon says it's okay to ask someone for help if you don't know how to do something because nobody knows how to do everything. You can go to lessons to learn how to take care of your baby, like you can go to lessons to learn how to do cooking or singing or makeup. It is called parent craft and they teach you how to do baths, dressing the baby and feeding it. I know because Joan told me that her sister had to do it when she had her baby. Her baby is called Sam and he is a boy and Joan is his auntie and she loves him but she wishes she had her own baby.

Marilyn Monroe would feed Issy by herself and not let a nanny do it. She would try to feed Issy from milk out of her breast but if it was too hard or it hurt or it didn't come out properly or Issy cried then she might get a bottle of milk instead. Sharon says if something is too hard, then you can find another way to do it that you find easier. Like if you try to use the clock to work out the time and you can't do it then you can work things out by putting your dinner in the oven at the start of *Coronation Street* and it will be ready at the end. Sharon says where there's a will, there's a way. She says there is always a way.

Marilyn Monroe might be scared of Issy and not always know what to do but she would always do her best and her best would be good enough. Sharon says you can only do your best. It is okay to make mistakes. Sharon says you don't have to perfect, you just have to be good enough. When Billy got upset because his pizza didn't look like the picture, Sharon said that it didn't matter. But I don't think some mistakes are okay, like if you burn your baby on the iron or you hit your baby when she cries or you let her head go under the water in the bath. If you make mistakes like that then Social Services will take your baby away and give it to new parents to look after because it means you are not good enough. I think my best would be good enough and I would be a good mother too.

My baby would be a girl and she would be called Janey. But if my baby didn't like her name, I would let her change it when she was old enough. I would let her pick her own name that she likes and I would stop calling her Janey and start calling her by her other name. My name is Marilyn and I don't like people calling me Jane because that is not my name any more. My baby, Janey might not want to change her name because she might be happy with the name I gave her and happy with me and she wouldn't have to live with foster parents because she could live with me.

I would make sure that I asked Sharon for help with parent craft and that I learned all the things you have to know to look after a baby because I am okay at learning. I have learned lots and lots of new things at the day centre like how to cook pizzas and how to work out time and how to do personal hygiene and makeup and money. And I have learned

130

lots and lots of new things at Cranley Crescent like how to do shopping and change my bed sheets and sort out my washing. Some of the things Natasha helped me to learn and some of the things I learned by myself like using colours because that makes it easy. Some things I learned by accident like when I burned the toast so I turned the knob down and tried it again and it came out better.

Natasha has come back in the bathroom now and she is holding the stick that I weed on and she is looking at it, to work out the answer.

I am sitting on the toilet with the lid down and my clothes pulled back up, waiting for the answer. I don't like waiting.

Janey is still standing by the bathroom door. Her eyes are very big and she looks sad. She looks like she doesn't know what to do.

Natasha looks at me and I know what the answer is.

I would have been a good mother. But it doesn't matter now because I am not having a baby. The test said that I am not having a baby and tests are always right. Tests always tell you if you are wrong or right. And it told me that I am wrong. I am not having a baby, after all.

'You're not pregnant, Marilyn,' says Natasha

Janey comes over to me and she puts her hand in my hand and a tear rolls down her cheek. She would have been my baby and I would have been a good mother. She climbs up onto my lap and I cuddle her tight.

27

Today, I am going back to Dagenham.

Today, I don't smile at the person sitting opposite me on the train. It is a man. He has black hair and it is greased back with lots of gel and it looks like slime and it makes me feel sick. He has a black briefcase on the seat next to him and he is pretending to read his paper but really he is looking at me. His paper is so big that he could hide behind it, if he wanted to. But he doesn't. He puts the paper on the table and pretends to read it. I am looking out of the window. Everything is moving very fast, so all the colours are mixed up. Trees look blue and sky looks green and pavement disappears.

I am looking out of the window with my eyes but I can still see him looking at me. I don't know how because my eyes are not looking at him. I can feel it. My face feels hot and I want to put some water on it to make it feel better. I have got my handbag and I have got some money that Seb gave me because Natasha said she better not give me any money because she might get in more trouble with Rose about it. I think it's stupid because why should she get in trouble for helping me?

Today, I am going back to Dagenham to Mum and Steve's, even though I don't want to, because Natasha said I couldn't live with her. She is not my friend. She is not my support worker. This morning, she got Seb to cook me scrambled eggs on toast. He is better at cooking than her. She is not that good at cooking even though she has to help other people do cooking. She is quite good at birthday cakes and beans on toast but that's all. She is not good at scrambled eggs because she burns them on the bottom of the pan.

I think the man with the slimy hair has stopped looking because I can't feel his eyes on my face any more but I still want to put some water on my face but I don't want someone else to take my seat. If you don't want someone to take your seat, you have to leave something on it so they can't sit there. If you leave something on it, you have to ask someone to keep an eye on it. It means they have to keep their eyes looking at it, to stop someone sitting on it. You can't keep one eye looking at it because both your eyes have to look at the same thing unless you close one eye, then you could keep one eye on it but that would be silly.

'Excuse me?' I ask the man with the slimy hair.

He looks at me and he goes red like he needs to put some water on his face too.

'Yes?'

'Can you keep an eye on my bag, please?'

I can see red dots on his neck.

'Your bag?'

'Yes, my bag. Can you keep an eye on it, so I can go to the toilet and no-one else can take my seat? Please.'

I nearly forgot to say please that time but it is important to say please because it is manners. It is important to have manners because it is polite. It is important to be polite because it is.

The man with the slimy hair smiles at me. His teeth look like they are slimy, as well as his hair.

'Sure. I can keep an eye on your bag, so no-one takes your seat.'

I might have to vomit in the toilet if he keeps talking because he makes me feel sick. Lots of men make me feel sick. Like Steve and the men in the kitchen. Like Zig in *MacDonalds*. Like the boys in white trainers. White trainers. Blue car. White van. Black dog. Brown collar. A woman in a long coat. It was grey. The coat was grey. But not Wesley. Wesley makes me feel happy. And not Patrick. Patrick is okay. And not the Chinese man behind the counter, whose daughter is Mai, because he talks to me in a nice way and gives me free spring rolls.

Last night, Natasha said I should probably ring Rose but I

133

don't think she wanted me to ring Rose from her house, really. I don't think she likes Rose, really. I think she is scared of Rose. Rose looks like a rose with red hair but roses have thorns and thorns can hurt you. Natasha said I should ring Mum, to let her know I am okay but I don't think she wanted me to ring Mum from her house, really. I think she is scared of getting in more trouble. I didn't want to ring Mum but I did ring because Natasha said if I didn't, then Mum might ring Rose and report me missing and then both of us might get into lots of trouble and it might make it harder for me to get back to my flat in Cranley Crescent.

I rang Mum but I didn't tell her I was at Natasha's house. I said, 'Mum, I am okay, so don't worry. I am coming home tomorrow.' I don't think Natasha had to worry about Mum ringing Rose and reporting me missing because Mum just said, 'Oh, okay. Jane?' and I think she dropped the phone. I could hear the bottle people crashing. When I think about all those bottles, I don't want to go back to Mum and Steve's house. When I think about Steve, I feel sick.

I go to the toilet and I turn on the cold tap. I know it is the cold tap because it has a blue top. Blue is for cold and red is for hot like red hot chillies or red fire but that's not really red, it's orange or sometimes it is even blue so it is quite confusing. I turn on the cold tap and I put my hands under it and fill them up with water, like a bowl and put it on my face. I look at my face in the mirror and it looks horrible. It looks so horrible. I never knew how horrible it looked before.

There is a line that goes from next to my eye to just above my lips. It is jagged and red and horrible. It is so horrible. There is another line on top on my eyelid. It is small but it is still horrible. There are more marks on my cheek. The marks look like someone's shoe. And there is a round shape on my neck where the skin has gone dark in the middle and white on the edge. It is called scars. It looks so horrible. The doctor said that the scars were healing very nicely. Much better than he would have dared imagine. I'm a very lucky girl. I think he was pretending.

Sometimes, people pretend to make you feel better. It is called a white lie. Like when I told Billy that his shirt was nice when I thought it was horrible because it has horrible colours on it that I don't like, which was khaki and turquoise. Khaki is a horrible colour because it is half between green and brown and it looks like poo. Turquoise is between green and blue and it makes my eyes hurt. Khaki and turquoise together are very bad. Khaki and turquoise together in stripes are very, very bad. But I didn't tell Billy his shirt was very, very bad. I told him it was nice because I wanted him to feel nice but it was a lie.

I dry my face on a paper towel but it is more like paper than a towel because it is hard and scratchy and it makes my face more red. I wish I had my handbag and it wasn't sitting on my seat with the slimy man's eyes on it because I have lipstick and mascara and powder in my handbag and I want to put it on. I have a brush in my handbag and I want to brush my hair.

Natasha asked me lots of questions after we did the test. She asked me if it was good news or bad news. I felt bad. I would have been a good mother. But I stopped feeling so scared because the test said I wasn't pregnant and that means they couldn't kill my baby or take it away. Natasha asked me about Wesley and whether we were still seeing each other. I told her that we went to the cinema and I wanted to show her the photographs of me and Wesley and Patrick but I remembered that Steve picked them up off the kitchen floor so I couldn't.

She asked me whether I was going to get my injection done again when I got back to Dagenham or whether I wanted to arrange to see Doctor Singer again. I said I would see Doctor Singer because she is nice and because I know how to get the train to Southend and anyway, I am coming back to Southend when Rose has sorted things out and found Karen a flat of her own and then Joan will be my best friend again.

28

The man with the slimy hair and teeth smiled at me with his slimy teeth, when I got off the train. Today, I am going back to Dagenham to Mum and Steve's, even though I don't want to. Rose said I don't have to do anything I don't want to do because I am an adult and I can make my own choices. I don't want to go back to Mum and Steve's. I want to eat some chips. I like chips. With red ketchup. I want to eat a spring roll and chips.

I go to the fish and chip shop with the orange sun on the window and the Chinese man behind the counter, whose daughter is Mai, but he is not there. There is a Chinese woman behind the counter. I have seen her before in the kitchen but not behind the counter. I think she is married to the Chinese man.

'Hello?' she says. Her voice in high and quiet. I have never heard her speak to me before.

I feel like I have been away for ages and ages and ages.

'Can I have a spring roll and chips, please?' I ask.

'One spring roll chips,' says the woman.

She asks for the money and I open my hand bag to get the money that Seb gave me. He gave me a twenty pound note, so I know that will be more than enough. I think notes are better than coins because you don't have to worry about counting it all out if you just give a note and get the change back. There is a card on the top of my purse that I didn't put in my bag. I look at the card. It has words and numbers printed on one side and biro writing on one side. The writing says, C A L L   M E. I think the man with the slimy hair and teeth must have put it in my bag when I went to put water on my face because no-one else could have done it if he was keeping his eyes on the bag.

Maybe he took his eyes off the bag and started reading the paper, though and someone else put it in there. But I didn't see anyone else looking at me like he was looking at me.

'Thank you,' I say to the woman when she gives me the change because it is important to be polite.

I have to see Wesley, now.

'Marilyn,' says Wesley when he opens the door.

He is wearing tracksuit bottoms but no top and he looks sexy. He is rubbing his eyes with his hand. He looks tired, like he has just got out of bed.

'Is it early?' I ask him but I don't think it can be that early because I had scrambled eggs for breakfast and then I got the train and then I had spring roll chips for lunch.

'Nah, no, it's not early. I'm just knackered.'

'Can I come in then?'

'Yeah, yeah. I'm really knackered, though, Marilyn. I think I might need to go back to bed and sleep.'

'I could come back to bed with you,' I say.

He closes the door and we are in the hall. I start taking my clothes off. I take off my jacket. I take off my jeans. I take off my top.

'Marilyn! What you doing?' says Wesley but he can see what I'm doing.

'Babe, I need to sleep. Anyway Patrick's just gone to get some milk. He's coming back in a minute.'

'So?'

I take off my bra and I take off my knickers.

'Marilyn, put your clothes back on. I mean it.'

Wesley starts walking back to his bedroom and I walk behind him. I want him to look at me but he is not keeping his eyes on me.

I think it is good to be naked but people think it is rude. When you are born you are naked. You don't come out with clothes on. Animals walk around naked, except when people put clothes on them, like those tartan jackets you can put on dogs but that is stupid. Marilyn Monroe used to walk around her house naked all the time, even if other people were there, like makeup girls or other women or men even. It wasn't rude. She liked to walk around without her clothes on. I like it too. If you walk around without your clothes on with your boyfriend or your husband, then they are supposed to want to have sex with you.

Wesley gets back in the bed, with his tracksuit bottoms on. He is not keeping his eyes on me. He is keeping his eyes on the floor. I get in the bed with nothing on.

I start to kiss him but he isn't kissing back.

'What's wrong?' I ask him.

'Nothing,' he says.

'I thought you liked me?'

'I do like you.'

'I thought you loved me?'

'It's just getting a bit serious.'

Wesley didn't look happy in the photographs because Wesley is not happy with me, anymore. I get out of the bed and I am standing naked, next to the bed and now, Wesley has his eyes on me.

'Don't you love me anymore? Don't you want me anymore?' I ask him.

I feel his eyes looking at different parts of my body. I feel his eyes like I felt the eyes of the man with the slimy hair and teeth.

'Of course I want you,' he says.

I get back in the bad and I start to kiss him again and now, he is kissing me back and he is pulling off his tracksuit bottoms and his body is on my body.

'Marilyn, Marilyn...'

He is saying my name like he loves me again.

'We can have another baby,' I say.

Wesley stops saying my name and he moves his body off me.

'What?' he says.

'We can get married and have a baby because we love each other but we don't love each other too much,' I say.

138

'You said we can have another baby. What do you mean another baby?'

He is leaning up on his elbow. He is looking at me but not in the way the man with the slimy hair and teeth was. I think he is cross.

'I thought there was a baby but the test said there wasn't a baby but we can have another one, can't we?'

He is still looking at me and his eyes are moving very fast.

'We don't have to have a baby now,' I say.

He gets out of the bed and he puts his tracksuit bottoms back on.

'Marilyn, I don't want that! I'm sorry, I'm, I can't... I thought you were using something.'

'I was. I was on the injection. I can get another injection from Doctor Singer. We don't have to have a baby now.'

'Marilyn, I think you'd better go. I'm sorry, I don't need this right now.'

'I thought you loved me.'

I love Wesley.

I hate Wesley.

29

I take the card out of my bag and look at it. It has words and numbers on one side. I can't read all of the words but I can read some of the words. I can read the name, Mark because I know this name because there is someone called Mark at the day centre. He is staff and he runs groups with magazines and calendars and papers and you get a notebook. It is called improving reading skills but some people just look at the pictures in the magazines and calendars and papers and don't look at the words. Like, some people look at pictures of recipes in magazines and work it out without the words and some men look at pictures of girls with no clothes on, in newspapers. It is called page three but it might not be on page three, especially if it is in a magazine and the girls might be wearing funny clothes made of rubber. You are not allowed to take these magazines into Mark's group but I have seen some people with them anyway.

I don't want to go back to Mum and Steve's.

I can read the name Mark. I can read lots of names of people I know like Billy and Joan and Paul and Penny and Gillian and Frank and Sharon and Natasha and Rose because I learned it at the day centre. It is important to know how to read and write names of people that you know because then you can send them a Christmas card. The Mark on this card isn't Mark from the day centre. He is the man with the slimy hair and teeth. I turn the card over. The writing says, C A L L M E.

I don't want to go back to Mum and Steve's.

I can read some numbers like from one to ten and also nought. Nought looks like the letter, 'O' so you might get mixed up but if you see 'O' with other numbers, you know it is meant to be a nought. Like if it is a phone number then you know it is a nought. The number on the card is a phone number but there are three different lines of numbers.

I don't want to go back to Mum and Steve's.

I thought Wesley and me were going to get married and have a baby and I could live there.

I don't want to go back to Mum and Steve's.

I walk back past the fish and chip shop with the orange sun on the window and the woman who is married to the Chinese man. I wave at her and she waves back. Where is the Chinese man? Maybe he decided that he didn't love her anymore, like Wesley decided that he didn't love me anymore. I have decided that I don't love Wesley anymore. I will love the man with the slimy hair and teeth.

I don't want to go back to Mum and Steve's.

I go to the phone box and I put some coins in and then, I press all the buttons for the first line of numbers. It used to be hard to use a payphone because there are so many things to remember like where to put the money and how to do the numbers but Natasha showed me how to use pay phones and it's not hard any more. The number isn't ringing properly. It is making a strange noise. I don't think I have done it right, so maybe it is still hard to use a payphone.

I put the phone back on the place where it goes and the coins come out the bottom.

I start again and I press all the buttons for the second line of numbers and it rings properly.

'Hello, Mark Sutton speaking,' says the man with the slimy hair and teeth.

'Hello, Marilyn speaking,' I say.

'Who?' he says.

There are lots of noises in the background like cars.

'My name is Marilyn.'

'Who is this?' he asks but then the phone goes dead.

I put some more money in and I press all the buttons for the third line of numbers and it rings properly and then someone answers.

'Hello…'

It is Mark.

'Hello. This is Marilyn,' I say.

'... through to the answer phone for Mark and Sarah Sutton. We're sorry we can't take your call right now but please leave your name and number and we'll get right back to you.'

There is a beep.

'Hello,' I say. 'My name is Marilyn. You said to call you so I am calling you.'

I put the phone back on the place where it goes. No money comes out.

I put some more coins in and I press all the buttons for the second line of numbers again.

'Hello, Mark Sutton speaking,' says the man with the slimy hair and teeth.

'My name is Marilyn. I met you on the train. You kept an eye on my bag and you put a card in it. It said to call you, so I am calling you.'

'Ah,' he says. 'Marilyn. Of course. Like Marilyn Monroe. That's your name.'

'Yes. My name is Marilyn, like Marilyn Monroe.'

'Where are you, Marilyn?'

'I am in Dagenham by the fish and chip shop with the orange sun on the window.'

'I see. I see. Would you like to meet me now?'

'Okay.'

'Good. Good, Marilyn. I can meet you in the alleyway by the station, in half an hour.'

I don't want to meet in the alleyway. It smells.

I don't want to go back to Mum and Steve's.

Wesley does not love me anymore.

'Okay.'

.

Bus Stop (Revisited)

30

I am at Heathway station. A man in a stripy suit is talking into a mobile phone and walking round in circles. Once I saw a monkey do that in the zoo. It was a trip that Sharon organised. I thought it would be good to go to the zoo and see lots of animals because I like animals. But it wasn't good. It was sad. The most sad thing was the monkey that walked round in circles. Sharon said it because they got bored being in a cage, with nowhere to go. Sometimes, I get bored, even though I don't live in a cage. I live in a flat in Cranley Crescent. I live in a flat that Karen is in.

I don't want to go back to Mum and Steve's.

I see the photo booth where Wesley and Patrick and me had our photos taken. Maybe I can get a picture taken with Mark when I meet him in the alleyway. Mark is my new boyfriend. If we love each other, we can get married and have a baby. Mark's phone said Mark and Sarah. I don't know who Sarah is. She might be his mum or his sister. If she is his wife, we can't get married until he gets divorced. Marilyn Monroe got divorced with Jimmy or Joe, so I don't think it is bad, even though Mum says it is against the church but she's not married, so it doesn't count.

If you go out with a married man, it has to be a secret. Nobody is allowed to find out. That's what Mr Williams told me at school, when I was Jane. He loved me very much but he couldn't get divorced because his wife would take him to the cleaners. I don't know why because he wasn't dirty but he did like to say dirty things. I told my friend Cherie what he said and she said it was dirty talk. I haven't seen Cherie for a long time. I don't know where she lives now.

Mr Williams loved me very much but it had to be a secret because I would get into trouble if anyone found out and I wouldn't be allowed to see him again and I wouldn't be allowed to stay at Cannon School. I would have to go to a school where you live all the time and they lock you up and never let you out. I didn't tell anyone except for Cherie. I made her promise not to tell anyone or else I would tell on her about her boyfriend from the park.

Mr Williams had black hair but some hair was missing. It is called a bald spot. But he didn't shave it off like Johnny. He liked to comb it over so it was long on one side and it would fall down when he was doing things to me in the store cupboard and he looked funny. Mark has slimy hair but Sharon says you shouldn't judge a person by what they look like because beauty is only skin deep. I liked looking at Wesley more than Mark, though. Mark said I am meeting him in half an hour but I don't know when he said it.

I come out of the station. A bus stops at the bus stop. Lots of buses stop here. There was no bus at the bus stop on Christmas Eve. It was not this bus stop. I waited but there was no bus. I can see the alleyway from here, but I can't see Mark unless he is inside. Alleyways are places that you can hide, like store cupboards and men's toilets and subways after dark.

Mr Williams said I was his special girl and he loved me very much because I was the prettiest girl in the school. I don't think I was pretty when I was Jane because I had mousy brown hair and big glasses and I wore a horrible green uniform and knee socks. I used to call him Daddy because I never had a Daddy and because he asked me to. My first boyfriend was Sam. He was my boyfriend when I was five and we held hands in the playground. I wasn't allowed to hold Mr Williams' hand in the playground because it was our special secret.

Mark is walking to the alleyway. I don't think he has seen me because his eyes are not looking at me. They are looking at nothing, like he is thinking. If you are thinking, your eyes might not be able to look at anything because they might be looking inside your head. He is quite good looking but I don't like his hair or his teeth. I watch his back as he walks into the

146

alleyway and then I can't see him anymore.

Another bus stops at the bus stop. The stripy man is getting on the bus and he is still talking to his phone. A boy is standing at the bus stop. He is wearing a hood. It is green. Another boy is sitting next to him. He is wearing a hood. It is black. They are wearing trainers. White trainers. Blue car. White van. Small fluffy black dog. Brown collar. A woman in a long coat. It is grey. The coat is grey.

I don't want to go back to Mum and Steve's.

Wesley does not love me anymore.

I walk to the alleyway and I follow Mark's back. He is wearing a grey coat with hairs on it. He stops walking and turns round and then he sees me and smiles. I don't like his teeth.

'Hello, Marilyn,' he says.

'Hello,' I say.

'Aren't you going to come closer?' he says.

I do what he says.

He puts his arms around me and starts to kiss me. His mouth tastes horrible like bad apples that have gone mouldy. He puts his hands inside my coat and up my jumper.

If you have sex with your husband or someone you love and who loves you, it's called making love. If someone does it to you and you don't want it, it's called rape. This is what Sharon told me in safety class. Sharon does lots of different classes like cooking and singing and hair and make-up. Sharon came to see me at hospital. I like Sharon. I want Sharon to be here.

He pulls at my clothes and puts his hands inside my knickers.

Sharon says it is important to avoid getting yourself into difficult situations with men. She says that you shouldn't meet up with a man that you don't know on your own. She says that you should only meet in a public place to be safe or in a group.

He is having sex with me but it doesn't feel right. I think

147

he has put it in the wrong hole.

Sharon says that if you are going out with a man it is important to make it clear at the beginning how far you want to go. Sharon says you are in charge of your own body and no-one else can tell you what to do with it.

It hurts and I don't like it.

Sharon says that sometimes men might want to do things that you are not ready for. Sharon says it is important not to let anyone force you into doing anything that you are not ready for. Sharon says every woman has the right to say no. In safety class we did role play, which is pretending. I was pretending to be the girl and Billy was pretending to be the boy and he asked me if I wanted to go back to his house and go to his bedroom with him and I had to say no I do not want to do that but we can go to the cinema with some other friends. Then we picked the film and said we would all go together after the day centre and we really did go to the cinema even though it was pretending first.

It hurts but I don't say no.

'Do you want to meet me again, tomorrow?' Mark says.

He has horrible slimy hair and horrible slimy teeth and he is horrible and he is not my boyfriend and he does not love me and I don't love him back.

'No!' I say. I say it loud. But it's too late because we had sex already.

31

Marilyn Monroe started writing a book about her life but she never finished it. It is called an autobiography. If someone else writes a book about you it is called a biography. Natasha told me that. Joan likes to collect books about people even though she can't read all the words. She has got books on Princess Diana, Geri Halliwell, Robbie Williams and David Beckham. I like to collect books about Marilyn Monroe. I have lots of books about Marilyn Monroe. Natasha used to read them to me and we would look at the pictures together.

You can write an autobiography about yourself even if you are not famous. It is called a diary but it is different to a diary that you put appointments in like a calendar. I have a diary for appointments and I have a diary where I can write or draw what I have done that day, or how I feel, or anything I want. I bought it with Sharon and it has red flowers on the front. Sharon told us about keeping a diary and then we all went and bought one. Sharon said we didn't have to keep a diary but some people find it helps them. Billy likes to draw pictures in his diary. He showed me some of the pages. When he made a pizza and cut his hand, he drew a picture of his hand with red pen to show the blood.

I haven't written in my diary for a long time. I want to put something in my diary now because I feel bad. It is in my flat in Cranley Crescent. I have a pen in my bag and I have the card that Mark gave me. I have stopped running and I am sitting in the photo booth. I put the card on my lap and I find the word that says M A R K. I put the pen on top of the word and I draw on it until I can't see the word anymore, then I dig the pen in hard and the card breaks. I pick up the card and there is ink on my jeans. I turn the card over and I start drawing. I draw a face with big slimy teeth. I scribble it out until the ink comes through again.

I hate him.

Someone pulls back the curtain. It is a man with red cheeks and a little boy.

'Are you finished in there, love?' he says.

I screw up the card and throw it on the floor and I get out of the man's way. The little boy looks like him. He has red cheeks too.

I am walking but I don't know where I am going.

I walk back past the fish and chip shop with the orange sun and I look in the window to see who is there. The Chinese man behind the counter, whose daughter is Mai, is back and I wave at him.

I don't want to go back to Mum and Steve's.

There is nowhere else to go.

I am on the doorstep of Mum and Steve's house. I knock on the door but no-one answers. I look under the brick hidden in the bush that Steve is supposed to trim but never does. But the key isn't there. I don't have my own key. I had my own key at Cranley Crescent and I liked it. I had it on my Marilyn Monroe key ring and it made me happy to see it every time I opened the front door.

I go to the front window and try to look into the living room but I can't see anything because the curtains are shut. I don't know what time it is because I have got confused but I don't think it is night time. Maybe Mum is having a nap on the sofa. She likes to sleep in the afternoon, sometimes. I bang on the window to wake her up and I go back to the front door but she doesn't come.

Janey pushes open the letter box and looks inside. I look inside next to her. I start coughing because it smells so bad. I take my head away and smell the bush. It smells green. I pull off a leaf and put it over my nose. Then I look back through. I can see lots and lots of letters on the floor. Some of them have footprints on like someone has walked over them. I can see lots of different rubbish in the hall. Crisp packets. Pizza boxes. Beer cans. All the bottle people. I am hungry and I want a pizza. Mum's dressing gown is in a ball at the end of the hall. It looks dirty.

I start to cry because I don't know what to do. I wish I was back at Cranley Crescent because at least I could press the star button on the phone and someone would be there. I could go back to the phone box. I don't want to speak to Mark again. I want to talk to Natasha. I don't have her phone number. I sit on the doorstep and curl myself up. I pretend I am a ball. Janey sits next to me and we wait.

I don't know how long we wait but I think it might be a long time because when I stop being a ball, my neck hurts. Janey is standing up and she is pulling my hand like she wants to show me something. I look up. A woman is pushing a pushchair along the pavement. She has got black hair with red in it and she is wearing a very tight red top that makes her arms look like sausages. I can't see the baby. Janey waves at her and she stops.

'You okay, love?' she asks.

I think she is talking to Janey so I don't answer.

She pushes the gate.

'Excuse me,' she says. 'You alright?'

Now I can see the baby. Janey goes over and strokes the baby's curly black hair. I would like to touch the baby. Its hair looks like fur and it has big brown eyes. Its skin is like coffee. I don't know if it is a boy or a girl but it is beautiful and it makes me want to cry again. If Wesley and me had a baby, it would look like that, but Wesley and me aren't going to have a baby. Wesley doesn't love me anymore.

The baby starts screaming.

'Shh, shh now,' says the woman.

She bends over and picks it up with her sausage arms. She jigs the baby up and down and smiles at it. It is wearing a baby suit with bunny rabbits on it. Janey holds onto the pushchair.

'She's teething,' she says to me.

The baby is a girl.

'She's lovely,' I say. 'What's her name?'

'Jasmine,' says the woman. She looks at Jasmine and puts on a silly voice, 'Yes, you are, ain't you?'

'Look, love, I don't mean to pry, but everything okay? You look a bit, you know…'

I don't know.

Jasmine has grabbed hold of a bit of red hair and put it in her mouth.

'You Ange's daughter, ain't you?'

I nod. I see tears fall onto my knees.

'I don't wanna talk out of turn but Ange's been looking a bit rough herself lately. You know what I mean? Black and blue, she was. That fella of hers is no good. I told her before. She won't listen. Can't you talk to her?'

'No,' I say.

'Used to see her down the club every Friday but not for ages now. He don't like her going out, does he? Ah, shame. Some women like 'em like that. What can you do, eh?'

'I don't know,' I say and I pull my knees in. I think I want to be a ball again.

'Well, if there's nothing I can do…'

Jasmine has stopped crying. Jasmine's mum puts her back in the pushchair and looks at me.

'I'm Max, by the way,' she says and puts out her hand. Her skin looks dry and flaky. She is wearing a silver ring with a big red stone. 'From number twelve.'

I put my hand up to her hand. It feels rough. Janey runs back over to me and holds my other hand.

'Well, if you need anything.' She takes her hand away and pushes Jasmine through the gate.

When they are gone, Janey pulls me up and she takes me to see the Chinese man, whose daughter is Mai.

32

'Watch where yer going, bitch!'

A boy is looking at me like he hates me. His eyes are small and red and watery. His friend is laughing. His mouth is open. I can see his fillings. He has lots of fillings. I can see his chewing gum stuck to his fillings. They are wearing hoods. Green hoods, black hoods, red hoods, yellow hoods. So many colour hoods. There are too many people in the high street. Janey is pulling me up to go to the chip shop, to see the Chinese man, whose daughter is Mai. I don't know if I can walk. I want a drink. I feel dizzy. I look down. He is wearing white trainers.

White trainers. Blue car. White van. Small fluffy black dog. Brown collar. A woman in a long coat. It is grey. The coat is grey. It is grey with black fluffy bits around the top. It is a scarf. A black scarf. She walks past but she doesn't stop. She looks at the floor. She walks fast.

'I bet you like it up the arse, don't you?'

But I didn't like it. I didn't like it at all.

'I said, watch where yer going, bitch.'

The one in the green hood is laughing. He spits out his gum and it lands on my arm. I feel sick.

'She's not fucking listening. What are you fucking looking at, huh? Huh, bitch.'

They are all laughing at the same time and making noises that scare me. Different colour eyes. Different colour skin. Different colour clothes. So many colours.

'We seen you before. Yeah. We seen you.'

'All on your own, now?'

'Where's your little friends, tonight, then?'

He smells like vinegar. Salt and vinegar. I am going to the chip shop to see the Chinese man whose daughter is Mai. I would like to meet Mai and ask her if she wants to be my friend.

White van. Blue car. The blue car stops at the traffic lights. There are girls in the blue car. One has long blonde hair and a silver top, like she is going to a party. She is holding the steering wheel tight with one hand. I am going to a party for Christmas Eve. I am going to meet Keith in my gold dress. I painted on a beauty spot just like Marilyn Monroe. There will be music and I will be dancing in my new gold sandals. Natasha said my feet would be cold in my gold sandals, but I wore tights and they don't feel cold.

The girl is smoking a cigarette with the window open. She lets go of the steering wheel and puts her arm out of the window. There is a tattoo on her shoulder. I can't see the picture properly. It looks like a dolphin. She looks out of the window at me. Her eyes look at my eyes. Her friend says something and she laughs and looks back at her friend. Her friend has curly hair. I put my curlers in with Natasha. She wanted to leave a bit early. She is supposed to stay until seven o'clock on Thursdays. She is not allowed to leave early. Just this once. It was Christmas Eve. Go on, Marilyn. You don't mind, do you? My hair will come out just fine, she promises.

I am supposed to get the bus with Joan and Paul and Penny and Gillian. They aren't here. I am too late because I couldn't get my curlers out on my own. One got caught in my hair underneath. It wouldn't come out. The hair was all tangled up and it hurt when I tried to pull it out. I was going to press the star button and make Natasha come back but I didn't. Just this once. I got the scissors and I cut it off.

The traffic light goes green and the girls are gone. The number plate starts with W. Red. Amber. Green. Only cross the road when there's a green man. It's important to learn your green cross code. To be safe. It's important to be safe.

'Get her, Bradley! Get her!'

An arm is round me. I don't know how it got there. It is grabbing me round the waist. I drop my bag. My lipstick falls

154

out into the road. A hand is round my mouth so I can't speak. I can't breathe. I can't breathe. I bite.

'Bitch!'

They drag me behind the bus stop where no-one can see. I don't know where the woman with the dog is now. There are lots of hands. Grabbing. I see blood. I don't feel anything. I see blood on my leg. I don't know whose blood it is. I see my gold sandal in the road. I see my tights on the ground. Then my face is on the pavement. It is black. It smells of dirt and stones. Someone treads on my hair.

33

When Marilyn Monroe died, she didn't have any clothes on. She liked to walk around her house naked. I do that too but I keep my slippers on because I don't want my feet to get dirty. I only do it at Cranley Crescent when I am on my own. Not at Mum and Steve's. If someone rings the doorbell, you don't have to let them in. You can go and get dressed first. But if you die, you won't be able to get dressed and everyone will see you naked. Mum says that you should always wear clean underwear, in case anything happens to you. You wouldn't want to collapse in the street and be wearing dirty knickers. My tights were on the ground. I don't know who saw me naked.

I don't want to die. Natasha read me a book once that said Marilyn Monroe ate a lot of pills and drunk lots of drink before she died. It said she died on a Saturday night but I don't know if she was going to a party like me. I don't know if she went to the hospital when she died or not. It said that Marilyn Monroe was killed but I don't know. Maybe she was killed by bad people, people like the boys in white trainers.

'Jane?'

I open my eyes. Mum is sitting by my bed wearing red lipstick. She is wearing Charlie Red again. I can smell it. I can smell drink, too. She is stroking my forehead.

'Jane, Jane, my poor baby, Jane.'

I look around. I am back in hospital but it is not the same as before. The curtains are white. They look new. I am in a ward with lots of beds. I don't have my own room.

'What happened?' I ask Mum.

'Don't you remember? You collapsed in the high street. Out cold, you were. That nice man from the chip shop found you and tried to wake you up.'

'Oh.'

A nurse walks past. She is not Gail.

'Mum, I want to go home. When can I go home?'
She holds my hand. She has a black eye. Her face has lots of different colours. Black, blue, purple, yellow. I can smell Charlie Red. I can smell drink too.
'I know, love. We're gonna have you back home in no time.'
'Not to your house. I don't want to go back there. I want to go back to my flat.'
Mum looks down. She lets go of my hand.
'I don't like Steve. He's horrible.'
She opens her mouth and closes it. She opens it again.
'I know, love. I know.'

If you have sex with your husband or someone you love and who loves you, it's called making love. If someone does it to you and you don't want it, it's called rape. I didn't say no because everything was black. Gail told me I was raped because the woman doctor who looked between my legs told her. I didn't like her doing that and I wouldn't open my legs and they had to give me an injection to calm me down, like the one they gave Joan, when they took her baby out of her. I don't think Gail would tell lies. Gail said that sometimes your mind can stop you remembering bad things but sometimes they come back. I would like to see Gail again and ask her if her mum has been staying in the spare room. But Gail doesn't work here. She works in the other hospital in Southend.

'How you doing, Marilyn?' asks Martha. She is my new nurse.

I am sitting in a room with just her and me and a table with flowers. They are pink and white.

'How can you tell the difference between a rose and a carnation?'

'Ah, well they are very different. They look different. They smell different. They feel different. Now these are roses. See the petals. Feel them. They're very soft. Can you feel that?'

She gives me a glass of water. I like water. Martha doesn't have red hair like Gail. She has brown hair and she wears blue eyeshadow. She has done special training. It is called counselling.

'When can I go home?'

'Just a bit longer now, my love. You've got to wait to see your social worker. Rose, isn't it? She's coming up from Southend to see you.'

'Oh.'

There are scratches on my hands. Martha says I got them when I fell on the pavement. I tell her it was black. She says the body has remarkable powers to protect itself. She says some of the same things that Gail said, like about your mind stopping you remembering bad things and about them coming back. I tell her that my mind remembers a lot of things. It can remember all the words to *'I Wanna be Loved by You'* and *'Diamonds are a Girl's Best Friend.'* I think my mind must have remarkable powers.

I tell Martha everything I remember. I tell her the boy's name was Bradley and I tell her about the girl with blonde hair and the silver top in the car. I tell her the car number started with W. I tell her the lady with the grey coat walked past with a small, fluffy black dog. I tell her that I don't know if my feet were cold or not. I tell her I didn't feel anything. I tell her I don't know what happened when it went black and the colours stopped. She says I might remember those things another day.

'But you might not. You might never remember any more because another possibility is that you might have been unconscious after that point. We'll just have to see.'

I don't think I want to remember those things. I think I want to be unconscious. Unconscious is like you are asleep or dead but only for a little while, then you wake up again.

Rose comes later and I tell her everything I told Martha. I tell her about Mum drinking all the time and about Steve. I tell her that I went to Southend and found Karen in my flat. I don't tell her what I did with Mark and I don't tell her I saw Natasha because I don't want to get in trouble.

'You've been very, very brave, Marilyn,' she says. She talks to me about going to the police. She says she can come with me and we can go to a special house with a video recorder and I can tell them everything there.

'But can't you just tell them what I told you?' I ask. 'I don't want to tell it again. I remembered it. Now I want to forget it.'

She tells me it's important because it might help the police catch them and stop them doing it to someone else.

'I'll go to that place if you let me have my flat back,' I say.

Something's Got to Give
(Unfinished)

34

Today is the first of June. It is Marilyn Monroe's birthday. I have a new Marilyn Monroe calendar on the wall and I have drawn a star in pink pen on today's date. I bought it from Southend market the day I got back and I bought a new pink candle too. Joan came with me. She is my best friend again. She bought five pairs of tights because she is doing a new job called work experience in an office and she has to wear tights. They were black and they had a pattern on them. She doesn't get paid any money to do the job but they said it would help her get a proper job. She said that would be very good and she is happy. I don't have a job yet but I go to the day centre and I have got my flat back, so I am happy too.

I did the thing Rose told me to in the special house with the video recorder and Karen moved into her own flat in Goodmayes. I didn't want to say it all again and the video recorder made me scared but then the woman called Ashleigh recorded herself talking into it first, to show me what to do and make me feel better.

'Today is the tenth of April two thousand and five,' she said. 'We are here to talk to Jane Marie Brown, who likes to be known as Marilyn.'

She nodded at me. I was happy that she got my name right even if she said I was Jane first. She played it back and we watched it on the telly. She was really good at it. I told her she could be one of those people that reads the news or the weather. I told her she would be really good at it because she talks nice and she looks nice on the telly. Her hair is the right kind of hair for that job. It is very smooth and shiny. She smiled at me and said it was my turn. I kept laughing, though, when I had to say my name. It is called introducing yourself. I felt stupid being on telly. I didn't want to do it wrong. She had to keep rewinding it and doing it again. She said it was okay. It was just practice. We could do it as many times as I wanted to.

I don't know how Marilyn Monroe did all those films because it is quite hard. It's a lot harder than you think it might be when you have a camera pointing at you and people looking at you. I said I had to go to the toilet and Ashleigh said that was okay and she took me to where the toilet was. The toilet paper was pink and that made me feel happy.

Rose was there but she didn't have to say much. Me and Ashleigh had the big parts. She was just a small part. Mum came too but she sat in the other room some of the time. When they do that on films it is called an understudy and the person just has to wait. If one of the actors is ill or they can't do it then the understudy can have a go instead. But Mum couldn't be my understudy because she didn't know the lines. I was the only person who could play my part because I knew all the lines. I had been through them lots of times, so I knew what to say. Janey was there too. She sat on the sofa next to me right at the start and held my hand. When I had to introduce myself she climbed into my lap. I thought that was nice but I had to tell her to go because she wasn't allowed on the film. I had to do it by myself.

When we came out, Mum put her arms round me and she cried really hard and she wouldn't stop crying. I was scared when she did that because I thought it meant something bad was happening but she said it was every mother's nightmare for her daughter to go through what I had been through. I didn't know what to say, so I asked if she wanted to get some chips.

The chip shop in Southend does better chips than the shop with the orange sun in Dagenham. We ate them walking down the pier and it made me think of Natasha and Seb. I looked in where the woman in the polka dot apron works and she was standing behind the counter like before, making tea.

'When are you going home?' I asked Mum.

Mum looked out to the sea and she looked like she wanted to be in the sea.

164

'Maybe I could stay with you for a bit,' she said.

I thought about Gail's mum sleeping in the spare room. I don't have a spare room.

'I could kip on the sofa,' said Mum.

I thought about the bottle people and it made my stomach hurt, so I didn't say anything but I looked at the sea too.

'Nah, I don't suppose you want your old mum cramping your style, do you?'

'Will you come to visit me again?' I asked. 'Like when I lived at Mummy Barbara's.'

'Yes, love. I'd like that.'

'Without Steve,' I added because I wouldn't like that.

'Without Steve,' said Mum.

I walked Mum to the station and she gave me a hug.

'Bye, Mum.'

She started crying again.

'Bye, Marilyn,' she said. She said it very quietly but it made me very happy that she called me Marilyn and not Jane.

Janey got up on tip toes and waved Mum goodbye as she walked down the platform.

Today, I am going to collect the birthday cake for the party. I have invited everyone. Joan and Paul, Penny and Gillian, Nigel and Frank, Billy and Sharon, Natasha and Seb. I even said to Mum on the phone yesterday that she could come if she didn't bring Steve. She said that Steve doesn't live there any more. He's gone. I didn't invite Wesley and Patrick because Wesley is not my boyfriend any more. I don't know if everyone will come but I hope they will.

Gita is helping me now. She helped me order the cake. She is my new support worker. She has long black hair and she wears jeans and boots with high heels and she laughs a lot. She is twenty-one years old. She is younger than me. She says she wants to be a social worker, so she has to get the experience because she did an English degree. That is why she is doing this job, even though the pay is crap. I ask her how much money it is and she tells me. It sounds like a lot of money to me. It is more than the Post Office give you. She says you get more when you are qualified but it's still not like being a doctor. She says that her parents don't want her to do it but she thinks it's still helping people, so what's the difference and anyway you can get good money if you get to team manager or whatever.

She is not like Natasha. She doesn't cry or talk about things that make her sad. She laughs a lot and she talks about university and she says everybody wants to be social workers now, if they can't get into medical school. She says everyone is looking for experience. You can't do anything without experience these days. I think she is right because lots of people want to be support workers. I have had lots of different support workers since I came back. They are called Agency. It means they might come for one day or one week or one month and you might not see them again.

Gita's friend, Saima is working in an old people's home but it is boring. Gita says it is better doing care in the community but she wouldn't want to work in mental health because you don't know what those people might do to you, do you? I mean, you hear all this stuff in the papers. She knows people who do child protection but they get burned out quick and that's not going to happen to her. She says learning disabilities is the easiest one and you get to go out and about. It's not so bad. She only has to do it for a year and then she can go back and do the training.

Gita pushes the door open and I go in behind her. Natasha used to always let me go first but Gita isn't Natasha.

'Ah, Marilyn Monroe, yes?' says the man behind the counter when Gita and me go in.

'I am Marilyn Brown,' I say. I thought everyone knew that Marilyn Monroe died but I am happy that he thought I was her.

'I think he means the cake,' whispers Gita and she laughs. Sharon says it is rude to whisper. I don't like it if she is laughing at me.

The man is staring at us. There is sweat running down his forehead. He better not get any on my cake or I am not paying him any money and I will make a complaint. Sharon says that you can make a complaint if you are not happy with the way you are treated or a service that is provided. She made a complaint to the bowling alley last week because some of the boys that served us drinks were laughing at Billy when he tripped over. It is not nice to laugh at people.

'Yes, that's it,' says Gita to the man.

When he turns round to get the cake, Gita whispers to me.

'Have you seen the sweat on that? It's disgusting serving food like that,' she says and she laughs at the man.

Sharon says it isn't nice to laugh at people. But Gita wriggles up her nose and she looks funny, so I laugh too.

35

'Ha haaaaaaaaaaaaaaaaaaaa!! A party. A party. We love parties, don't we Gillian? Party time! GILLIAN!!!!'

Penny and Gillian are early. I let them go in the lounge and I put my gold collection tape on so they can have some music.

Gita is still helping me get the food ready. Nobody was supposed to arrive for another ten minutes. We are putting everything out in bowls and plates in the kitchen. We have made bowls of crisps and nuts and plates of sandwiches and sausage rolls and little bits of pizza. We bought it all from *Sainsbury's* yesterday because Gita says it's easier than trying to make it all from fresh. She says there's no shame in buying convenience food. She says why make a pizza when you can buy one? Then you can have more time to have fun and have parties. I didn't tell her that Sharon says it is better to make your own food. Sharon says it is healthier and cheaper.

Penny is jumping up and down to the music and it is making her hair stick up even more than usual. She is wearing an old jumper with stains on, even though it is June and it is hot and even though it is a party. I am wearing a party dress but not my gold dress because I don't have that any more. I am wearing a red dress. It is very tight and very long and I have red shoes on and red lipstick. I look nice.

'Ha haaaaaaaaaaaaaaaa!!'

Penny is jumping higher and higher like she is on a bouncy castle like the ones you get on the seafront that children jump on. There is spit coming out of her mouth so I go back to the kitchen. Gillian follows me.

Gita and me bought paper napkins in red, green and blue and Gita helped me put them in the shape of a fan. It looks nice. The food is all neat and tidy. I have got the cake out of the box and put it on a silver plate in the middle. The picture is done with special icing. It is the one in the white dress, where it's blowing up in the air and she's laughing. But they have got her beauty spot on the wrong side. Mine is just right because I painted it on myself. They have done yellow icing for her hair and red for her lips and pink for her skin. She looks pretty. It is a shame that people will eat her.

'Oh,' says Gillian, looking at the cake. 'Oh.'

Gita is putting out plastic cups. She looks up at Gillian. Gillian is still staring at the cake.

'Ah,' says Gillian to the cake. 'Isn't she lovely.'

'Hello, Gillian,' says Gita.

'Oh. Hello. Who are you?'

'You remember me. I'm Gita. The new support worker.'

'Oh. Oh yes. Are you our new owner?'

'No, I'm not your owner, Gillian. Nobody owns you. I'm your support worker, remember? I came round to see you the other day. I'm here to help you. Remember?'

'Oh. Another one.'

Gillian walks up to Gita and strokes her hair.

'Ah, lovely hair. Hasn't she got lovely hair?' she says to me.

'Yes,' I say, because she has got lovely hair, and today she has put some glittery stuff in it for the party. It is called making an effort.

'Ah, she's nice. I like her. Will you do recipes with us?'

'Sure, Gillian. We can do recipes any time you like,' says Gita and she laughs. She laughs all the time. Penny laughs all the time too.

'Natasha does recipes with us,' says Gillian.

'Ha haaaa!! This music. This music. Ha haaaaaaa! Denise said we could, didn't she? Is Denise coming? Denise's coming soon. Where's Denise. Denise!!'

Penny runs into the kitchen and I am worried about the cake. Penny is coughing a lot and she sounds like she's got a bad throat. Her voice makes a horrible noise. There is lots of spit.

'You can wait in there, Penny,' I say. 'People will be here

169

soon.'

'Oh. Who's coming? Where's Denise? Denise!'

Denise was one of the Agency people but I don't think she is coming back.

'Penny, you can open the door to the guests,' I say. 'Would you like to do that? You can wait by the door, look.'

'Oh, the door. The door. Wait by the door. Better to wait. You have to wait, don't you? Yes. HA haaaaaa!!'

Then Joan and Paul arrive and Nigel and Frank and Billy and Sharon and there are so many people in my flat and it makes me happy. Penny looks happy too. She is jumping higher and higher.

Billy brought a big pack of lagers and Joan brought some wine. I don't drink alcohol because it tastes horrible but Billy and Joan and Paul are drinking it.

Billy is getting very loud.

'Good stuff. Good stuff, baby.'

'Er, Billy. Are you supposed to be drinking that?' asks Gita. She looks worried.

'Yes, I am,' says Billy and he turns his back on Gita.

'I just wondered about your medication. I don't think...'

'I'm an adult and I can make my own decisions!' Billy turns round and he shouts at Gita. 'You can't tell me what to do!'

'No, I... Em.'

Gita looks more worried.

'You can press the star button if you want,' I say.

'What? No, no. It's okay,' says Gita.

Mum isn't here yet. Natasha and Seb aren't here yet.

I dance to 'Diamonds are a Girl's Best Friend,' and I swing my necklace round. It isn't diamonds but it makes everyone laugh. I don't know what the time is but I start feeling tired and I am hot from all the dancing.

Penny is still by the door. I don't know how long she has been standing there. I don't know where Gillian is.

'Penny, come and dance!'

'I've got to open the door,' she says.

'No, come on.'

The doorbell rings again.

'DENISE!' screams Penny but I know it won't be Denise because I didn't even invite her to my party and Rose told me she's gone back to Australia.

'Maybe it's Natasha,' I say.

Billy hears me and he runs over.

'Ha, h-ha, ha. Natasha. Natasha, the gnat. Goodie, goodie, goodie.'

But it isn't Natasha. It's a boy called Jamie. I don't know him, but he says he is Billy's friend. He is very good looking and he has blond hair and big muscles so I let him in.

'I Wanna Be Loved By You' comes on, so I ask him to dance. He says yes and we dance and I lean my head on his shoulder and close my eyes. I think he likes me. I think he might be my new boyfriend.

I don't hear the doorbell go but when I open my eyes again Natasha is there with Seb and another man who I haven't seen before. I don't know if he is Seb's new boyfriend or Natasha's. She looks great. She has her hair all black with red streaks and she is wearing high black boots and a black dress and she has makeup on. Penny isn't by the door any more. I see someone else who I don't know, in my kitchen. Gillian is sitting staring at the cake.

'Oh my God, oh my God!' says Gita.

Billy is on the floor shaking.

36

Gita is not laughing any more. Natasha looks at Billy and talks to Gita in a low voice. Gita phones an ambulance because Billy isn't supposed to drink with his medication. He has epilepsy. It is when your brain doesn't work properly and you get fits and you shake and you might wet yourself or bite your tongue. Gita starts crying and Natasha puts her arm round her and presses the star button to talk to Rose. I didn't think Gita would cry about anything.

Natasha asks me if it's okay if we end the party now because Billy is ill. I say it is okay. Penny and Gillian and Joan and Paul go back to their flats. Nigel and Frank are gone already. Jamie says he hopes Billy is okay because Billy is his friend and he would like to see me again. This makes me very happy and I say yes he can see me again and he says how about tomorrow. I say okay and then he goes. Natasha talks to the other people who I don't know and asks them to leave. Natasha is making everything right. I think this means she will be my support worker again.

My front door is open and everything is happening quickly and everyone is gone. I am standing by the door, where Penny was standing before. There are peanuts on the floor. There is squashed cake and there is a cigarette trodden onto the carpet. I can see red on my wall in the hall. It looks like blood but I think it is wine because I didn't see anyone bleeding. I don't know where the wine came from. I can hear Gita crying in the kitchen and Natasha talking.

There is no air in the flat so I stand outside on the doorstep and breathe the air. It is still hot, even though it is dark.

Penny is pulling back her curtain and she is waving at me. I wave back and then Gillian comes to the window too. She is wearing her night dress. It is white with blue flowers. And she has a net cap over her hair like old people wear. Penny disappears from the window and Gillian stays there looking. I look down at my dress and it is all crumpled and has wet patches where I am sweaty. I want to have a bath in my own blue bath. I am glad that I am back home and not at hospital where you have to have a shower on a seat where someone else's dirty bum has been or at Mum and Steve's, where Steve comes in when I am in the bath.

I am sad that Billy has to go to the hospital because it is not nice being in hospital. They give you horrible food and you have to stay in your bed and people get your name wrong. But there are some nice people like Gail and Martha. I hope Billy will be okay. But I am happy now because Jamie is my boyfriend and Natasha is my support worker.

The ambulance comes for Billy. It turns into Cranley Crescent and I see lots of curtains moving. Penny is back at the window with Gillian and she is wearing her blue dressing gown and she has white cream all over her face. The blue light is flashing on top of the ambulance and it makes me feel sick. It stops outside Frank's house and a man and a woman get out. They are wearing green boiler suits and carrying a bag. The woman smiles at me and I tell them where Billy is. Natasha is behind me at the door now and she is taking the man and woman in green through to the kitchen.

I go back inside, but I sit in the lounge because I don't want to get in the way.

'Is there anything we can do, Marilyn?' asks Seb in the doorway.

The other man is standing next to him. He has a skinhead too. I think he might be his boyfriend because if he was the other kind of skinhead I don't think he would be here.

I look around. There are peanuts and cigarettes and cake and wine and crisps and cans and mess everywhere. Someone has started tidying because I can see a black bin bag with rubbish in it but they haven't finished. I think it must be someone that left like Penny and Gillian or maybe Joan. I don't know. I don't think it was Seb and the man because they are asking me what to do like they don't know how to tidy up without asking. It is important to keep your flat clean and tidy.

'You could help me clear up,' I say.

'Sure,' says Seb and he looks around.

'You could put the rubbish in that bag,' I tell him because I don't think he knows what to do.

'Yeah, sure,' he says and his face goes a bit red.

'What's your name?' I ask the man.

He is wearing jeans and a tight red tee-shirt that says a long word on it that I don't know.

'I'm Mark,' he says and I feel sick because of the other Mark.

'Hey, Marilyn. It's okay,' says Seb. 'Mark's my friend. He won't bite.'

But the other Mark did bite. He bit me on my neck.

'Is he your boyfriend?' I ask.

'Well,' says Seb and he goes red again.

The man and woman in green are taking Billy out of the flat.

'Will he be okay?' I ask the woman.

'I should think so,' she says and then they are gone.

Gita comes out of the kitchen. She has wiped her face but it is all streaky. Her hair is messy and the glitter is gone.

'It's okay,' says Natasha to Gita. 'I'll stay for a bit. I need to talk to Marilyn, anyway. You get off. You look exhausted.'

'I'll see you tomorrow then,' says Gita and she walks past me. She puts her hands on my shoulders. Her voice is quiet and she is not laughing. She looks young.

Then Gita is gone and it is just Seb and Mark and Natasha and me. Seb and Mark are tidying in the lounge and Natasha and me are in the kitchen. Natasha is already putting stuff in a black bag and she is tidying some food away on the side.

'Oh, look at the cake,' I say.

It has all been eaten except for the feet. They have eaten her head, her blonde hair, her body, her arms, her white dress

174

and part of her legs. I haven't eaten any.

'Can I have a bit?' I ask Natasha because she is in charge again.

'Of course you can have a bit, Marilyn. It's your cake! You don't have to ask me.'

'But you're in charge,' I say and she sits on a chair in the kitchen. 'Do you want a bit?'

'I better not,' she says. 'Still watching my weight.'

She is slim now. Her legs look nice in long boots.

'Marilyn, I have to tell you something,' she says and I think it might be bad but she sort of looks happy so I don't know.

'Yes?' I say and I start washing up the glasses in the sink. It is important to be clean and tidy.

'Why don't you sit down?' says Natasha.

'No. I want to do this,' I say.

'Okay,' says Natasha and she gets up and stands by me at the sink. 'I'll dry, shall I?'

I nod and she picks up the tea towel. It is the one with red squares. Her nails are painted black.

'Marilyn, I'm not coming back to work here, you know,' she says.

She is drying my favourite glass with Marilyn Monroe's face on the side. I hope she doesn't break it.

'I've decided to go back home to Scarborough for a while,' she says. 'To see my mum and my sister, Katie.'

'What is she like?' I ask.

'She's a bit like you,' she says and she puts the glass down and puts her hand on my hand. 'She's very special. I haven't been a great sister to her but I want to be.'

'Maybe you could go and get her and bring her here. Rose could get her a flat.'

I would like to meet Katie. She could be my friend.

'I don't think that will happen, Marilyn.'

'Oh.'

'To be honest, I don't know if I'm ever going to come back to Southend. I don't know what I'm going to do afterwards.

So I guess this is goodbye.'
I look at her eyes and she is crying and I am crying too. I like Natasha. She is not my friend. She is not my support worker. She is Natasha and she is okay. Sometimes, she is happy and sometimes, she is sad and sometimes, she makes mistakes and sometimes, she cries. She is a just a woman. Like me. And she is going now.

When everyone is gone, I put on a special song for Marilyn Monroe's birthday. It is called, 'Candle in The Wind'. I think I will ask Mum over for Sunday lunch, next week. I will ask Gita to help me do a roast. And we can have green peas and carrots and gravy.

I hope Billy will be okay.